Keisha

&

Trigga 2

A Gangster Love Story

LEO SULLIVAN

PORSCHA STERLING

Text LEOSULLIVAN to

22828 to join our mailing list!

To submit a manuscript for our review, email us at

leosullivanpresents@gmail.com

© *2015*

Published by Leo Sullivan Presents
www.leolsullivan.com

DEDICATION

This book is dedicated to everyone who reads our work to escape the realities of every day life. We put our all in what we do to entertain you!

ENJOY and BE ENTERTAINED!

ONE

Keisha sat staring at the space Trigga had been before he disappeared behind the doors of the elevator. There was an eerie silence that hung in the air. Then suddenly, it was like an explosion went off in her head as a million thoughts erupted in her mind. But one thought was loudest of them all.

BITCH, RUN!

Unwilling to waste any more time, Keisha bolted over to where she'd left her purse on the glass dining room table and snatched it up quickly. She checked inside to make sure that she had her cell phone and then charged towards the elevator. Although it was only about a thirty second wait until it came up, it felt like an eternity. As soon as the doors opened, she jumped inside and mashed the button to the lobby. Then she pounded the button to the second floor. If she went straight to the lobby, she might run into Trigga on his way back up. She would go to the second floor and then take the stairs down. That would also give her time to call Tish for a ride.

Once the elevator doors opened wide enough for her to slide her slender body outside, Keisha ran out with her cell phone in hand as she dialed Tish's number. Taking turns looking from the phone to her surroundings, she breathed heavily while trying to focus her mind.

"Hello?" Tish said groggily once she answered the phone.

"TISH! I need you to pick me up. I just sent you the address," Keisha told her. Grabbing the door to enter the staircase, she took one last look behind her before she went in and started stomping down the stairs.

"What the hell you talkin' about, Keesh? Pick you up...why?"

"Because I don't trust Trigga right now. I—I don't know what's goin' on and I need time to get my mind right and think this shit through. I'll explain it to you later. Just get your ass up and come get me!" Keisha hung up the phone before Tish could answer. Now she was at the base of the stairwell and facing the door to the lobby.

Opening it just enough to peek outside, she peered out the door to check for Trigga. He was nowhere to be found. It was late but there was still a lot of activity out of the doors. The restaurant in the hotel was still open and had a person playing live music, as a few patrons swayed back and forth at the bar.

Keisha closed the door again and took a deep breath. Before walking out she wanted to do one last thing. She pulled out her phone once more and called Tish.

"I'm on my way," Tish said as soon as she answered the phone. "I'll be there in five minutes."

"Thank you so much," Keisha responded. "I'll explain everything to you later."

"You safe?"

"Yes, I am."

"Good," Tish told her. "I'll text you when I get there."

Keisha ended the call and took a deep breath. Her brain was still filled with thoughts of Trigga. She didn't think that he wanted to kill her anymore because if he did, he could have. But he had a lot of shit that came with him. His own twin brother was in on the ambush. He'd almost killed her and even came to the hospital and to Lloyd's condo to finish the job. All this stuff she was going through was due to her connection to Trigga. He was sexy and they had a connection but he wasn't worth risking her life for. At the end of the day, she didn't really know him at all.

Pulling the door open, Keisha scanned the outside once more before stepping out. She walked briskly through the lobby, her eyes searching around frantically with each step. She was so preoccupied with looking for Trigga that she didn't realize when she ran straight into an older man holding a glass of wine.

"Oh, damn it!" the man exclaimed as he looked at the red wine droplets that spilled on the front of his beige shirt when Keisha collided with his arm.

"I'm so sorry," Keisha muttered to him as she rushed away towards the door.

The man shot her an angry scowl and opened his mouth to complain once more. Before he could, Keisha took off in a run and darted out the lobby doors, afraid that she would cause more attention to herself if she stayed a second longer.

***

Trigga sat down in a small armchair in the lobby as he tried to get his thoughts together. Too much was happening all at one time, and he needed a minute to think it through before he went up to his room to face Keisha again.

Mase was tryin' to kill me? he thought to himself. *Why would Mase—my brother…why would my brother try to kill me?*

No matter how much he tried to create a reasonable explanation for that, it wouldn't fit. He and Mase didn't have the best relationship but they had love, if nothing else. Or so he thought. They'd never been close but that was Mase's fault. No matter how much Trigga had tried to reach out to him, he would reject it. On top of that, they were polar opposites. Mase wanted to do nothing but party, drink and chase pussy while Trigga was more focused on bigger goals. He worked hard to stack his bread because he didn't want to be doing this shit all his life. At some point he wanted a wife, kids, a dog…normal shit.

"Young people are so damn disrespectful!" an older man barked in the middle of the lobby, interrupting his thoughts.

Trigga looked up and followed the man's stare to the hotel lobby doors. When he did, he saw a woman running out the doors; a woman who looked an awful lot like Keisha. Trigga jumped up from his seat by the elevators and took off running towards the door. The older man turned towards him when he heard the heavy sound of his footsteps approaching and Trigga knocked right into him.

"Hey!" the man yelled out. He staggered backwards right into a chair which made his knees buckle. Waving his hands in the air as if he were drowning on the deep end of a pool, he flopped into the seat and then scowled at Trigga as he continued moving.

Trigga didn't bother to say anything. His focus was on the door where he'd seen Keisha run through. She was trying to leave and he couldn't let her do that just yet. He had too many questions that he needed answered.

***

"Damn, Tish, please hurry," Keisha mumbled to herself as she ducked off on the side of the building. She was standing in what looked like an alley under a flickering lamp, while she batted gnats away from her face.

The streets were dimly lit by the streetlights, but the one that hovered over the area she stood was just barely shining its light and cast a long, dark shadow over her. It was both a blessing and a curse; she could barely be seen from her position in the alley but if someone tried to bother her, she wouldn't be able to wave for help.

Keisha jumped when her cell phone chimed. It was a text from Tish.

Pulling up now.

OK, Keisha texted back. *I'm around the corner from the bldg. in the alley.*

Keisha waited about two seconds and then she saw Tish's hunter green Camry pull into the alley. Her heart leaped in her chest and she ran to meet her. Her heel fell into a rocky hole in the asphalt, but she recovered quickly and headed to the passenger side with only a mild twinge of pain radiating through her ankle.

"Keisha! Where the fuck you goin'?"

Keisha froze at the sound of Trigga's voice. She turned slowly towards where she had heard his voice and focused in on his face. He didn't look angry at all, only confused. Seeing that she had halted in her escape, he ran over to where she was and stood right in front of her face.

"Where are you goin'?" he asked again with a deep frown on his face. His grey eyes seemed almost black as he glared at her. "You leavin'?"

"I'm goin' home! I don't want nothin' more to do with this bullshit!"

"Bullshit?" Trigga looked at her incredulously. "You just told me that my brother tried to kill you! To kill me! You just told me that and now you tryin' to run your ass up outta here and you think that shit is okay?"

"Ever since the day I met you, I been pulled up in your shit! I'm tired of it! I don't want to have to fight for my life or be involved in some shit that don't have nothin' to do wit' me!"

Keisha could feel the hot tears streaming down her face as she spoke. She was tired, frustrated and scared. She wanted to get to know Trigga…she was intrigued by him, but they could never be.

He was a bad boy and no matter how much that fascinated her about him, she wasn't cut out for that life any longer. She wanted to go to college and be a normal college student. She wanted to live her life.

"That day at the club wasn't the first time you met me," Trigga said to her slowly.

Keisha frowned at him and used her hand to rub the tears from her face. Trigga's expression changed suddenly and went totally blank. She couldn't read him. Before she could say anything, he continued.

"The first time I saw you, Keesh, you were high as fuck. You were standin' between some buildings wearing a fuckin' pair of mismatched shoes, lookin' like a damn junkie. I don't know if you had got hold to some really good shit or some really bad shit, but either way your ass was gone. I tried to help you and you kicked the shit out of me until you passed out. I looked in your purse and found a keycard and piece of paper with your hotel room number on it, and took you back to your room." Trigga stopped there and watched Keisha's face as understanding slowly seeped in.

"It was you?" she reached into the top part of her dress and pulled out a small wrinkled up piece of paper from her bra. Unfolding it, she held it up for him to see. "You wrote this note?"

Trigga squinted at it as he tried to decipher the smudged words on the paper. Then he nodded his head slowly.

"Yeah, I left you that. I wanted you to get yourself together."

"So all this time...*all this time* you've been keeping that from me! You knew and didn't mention it?"

Keisha started to get angry, but it was more so from her embarrassment at knowing that Trigga had been the man who'd found her when she was at her all-time worse. He was the one who had pity on her. He was her savior, but just thinking of how she must have looked and acted that day mortified her.

"Whoa, hol' up...I didn't know who you were until you started flippin' out on me again in the room. You don't look the same as you did that night. Excuse my words, but you looked like shit. Plus, your hair was longer," he added. "Being clean did some wonders for your ass because I could tell you was cute and all, but I had no idea you could turn into all this." Trigga looked pointedly at her to stress his words.

"Oh..." was all Kiesha could utter. She had no other words to say. This night had revealed so much to her that she felt like her brain would overload on the information. "Well, I still want to go home."

Trigga looked down and didn't say anything for a moment. Then he nodded his head. "Okay. You can go."

Keisha took one last look at him and then opened up the passenger door. Trigga grabbed the handle from her fingers and pulled it open for her as she got inside. Once she was in the car, he closed it firmly behind her and walked away. Keisha watched him through the side door mirror as he trekked back to the hotel. Then, feeling as if someone was staring a hole through the side of her head, she turned towards Tish.

"Bitch, you got some explain' to do," Tish muttered as she gazed at Keisha through sleepy eyes. "Y'all muthafuckas done dragged me out the bed then had a lover's spat in the middle of the damn street. This shit better than the damn movies."

Keisha shook her head and laid her head against the window as they drove off.

TWO

"Keesh…um, I think you gonna wanna see this."

Keisha groaned and rolled over in her bed at the sound of Tish's voice. It was the next morning and she could tell by the sunlight seeping through her blinds that she'd definitely overslept and was late for class. But she didn't intend on going anyways after the night she'd had so it didn't matter much. It was a good thing that she had made a friend who she shared three classes with and could get the assignments from.

"What, Tish?" Keisha asked, pulling a pillow over her head.

"Get your ass up and come see!"

Keisha groaned once more and pushed the pillow off her head, before sitting up in the bed. After blinking a few times to focus her eyes, she saw that Tish was standing in her room with her head to the blinds as she peeked out the window. Instantly, Keisha was jarred awake as the feeling of alarm took over her body.

"What is it?" Keisha asked in a hushed whisper. She pushed the covers off and crawled to the foot of the bed where Tish was. She turned towards the blinds, opened them a small amount and peeked out.

There, sitting right in front of her apartment, was an all-black Porsche SUV. Trigga was there.

"What the hell is he doin' here?" Keisha asked as she snatched away from the window.

Tish ran a hand through her hair as she pulled away and turned to Keisha. Then she sighed.

"I guess he's lookin' out for you. He's been there all night, I think, because he's in Gladys' parking space and she gets in 'round 2 a.m. but you see she had to park over on that side. I know she's mad as hell."

Keisha turned on her heels and grabbed a robe from the hook on her door and wrapped it over her body. She walked into the kitchen, poured some coffee into a mug and grabbed some creamer out of the refrigerator then poured some into the mug. As she stirred the hot liquid, Tish gawked at her.

"A nigga stalking this bitch and she tryin' to get her caffeine fix. I done seent it all!" Tish exclaimed with sarcasm.

"I'm makin' him some coffee before I go out to talk to him," Keisha informed her and rolled her eyes as Tish scoffed. She placed some toast in the toaster and then turned around to look at Tish.

"About what? This nigga is caught up in a lot of shit! His own brother was in on that ambush...what the hell you got to talk to him about?"

Sighing, Keisha grabbed an egg out of the refrigerator, cracked it on the counter and watched it as the inside spilled out slowly onto the heated frying pan she'd placed on the stove. The egg started to fry, she grabbed a spatula and poked at it.

"I need to know how he's going to handle it," Keisha answered. "Based on that, I'll make my plan on whether I can stay here or if I need to move. Even then, I don't know where the fuck I'll go. I don't have anyone."

"Heffa-"

"EXCEPT you," Keisha corrected herself. "I have no one but you."

She grabbed the toast out and started to place butter and jam on top of the lightly toasted bread. Then she scrambled the eggs and placed light seasoning on them. After thinking for a second, she decided to sprinkle some cheese on top.

"What about tellin' the cops?" Tish asked as she watched her.

Keisha shook her head and pulled the toast out of the toaster. "I don't trust them. At the hospital, when I didn't speak up about what they wanted, they started lookin' at me like I had parts in that shootin' shit. Plus, snitchin' on everyone would put me in a worse position. And it would implicate Trigga."

"Yeah, but you barely know that nigga. Maybe his ass needs to be implicated," Tish said giving her a shrug. Keisha looked out through the thin curtain on the kitchen window and focused in on Trigga's ride. The windows were tinted but she knew he was in there.

"No," was all she said. "He doesn't."

***

Tap! Tap! Tap!

Trigga jumped suddenly at the sound of the knocking on his window. He didn't even remember falling asleep. Glancing at the clock on the dash, he checked the time before looking out the window. It was Keisha and she was holding a plate of food and a coffee mug.

"Humph," Trigga laughed a little to himself as he looked at her. It was early but she still was beautiful. Chicks was always talking about "I woke up like dis" and knew damn well they woke up looking like a swamp creature from the depths of The Everglades. But Keisha actually did wake up flawless.

"Well, good morning, you," Trigga said when he rolled down the window. Keisha turned towards him and narrowed her eyes at him.

"So you stalkin' me now?" Keisha asked him. "Didn't I leave your ass at the hotel last night?"

Trigga gave her a serious look. "You said you wanted to leave so I let your poutin' ass leave. But I'm gonna make sure you're safe."

"I can handle my own," Keisha retorted, slightly lifting her cute button nose in the air and sniffing indignantly.

"Oh yeah?" Trigga smirked. "Lemme see how you handled them eggs first and then we'll talk more about that." Trigga eyed the plate; a simple breakfast of sunny side up eggs and toast with butter and jelly. She did her thing from the looks of it.

Keisha shot him a nervous look as she shuffled back and forth from foot to foot. "I—I hope you like it." She pushed the plate towards him through the window. "Do you drink coffee?"

"Do I look like a coffee drinking ass nigga?"

Keisha smiled. "Well, what you tryin' to say about coffee drinkin' ass niggas?"

Trigga returned her smile and reached for the coffee. "Not a damn thing. Give me that. Get your ass in the car so I can tell you what I think when I'm done."

Keisha walked slowly over to the passenger side and glanced over at the window in her bedroom. She could've sworn that she saw the blinds move suddenly.

Nosey ass, Trish, Keisha thought and rolled her eyes.

By the time that Keisha sat down in Trigga's SUV and closed the door behind her, he was already digging in to the food like he was starving. A smile spread across her face as she watched him eat.

"I told your ass I could cook," Keisha bragged as she sat back on the cool leather seats and looked at him.

"Naw," Trigga responded as he took a sip of coffee. "A nigga just hungry as hell."

Attitude flaring, Keisha sucked her teeth and Trigga laughed as he looked at her. "I'm just kidding. You a'ight but if you had messed this up, it would have been a damn shame."

"Well, if I had known you were going to be stalking me all night, I would have gotten up earlier to prepare something," Keisha said. Then she got silent and the smile disappeared from her face, as she thought about the reason for why Trigga was there. He got quiet too and seemed to retreat into his thoughts so she knew he was thinking about it also.

"What are you goin' to do about Mase?" Keisha asked him, after debating in her mind about whether or not she should bring up the fact that Trigga's own brother was trying to kill the both of them.

Trigga sighed and sat back on his seat. He placed the plate of half-eaten food down on his lap and rubbed his face with his hands.

"I gotta talk to him," he told her. "No offense, Keesh, but that's my brother. He's my twin brother. I can't just go off your word on something like that."

"I understand," Keisha said then looked out the window. She didn't have any siblings but she could imagine that if someone had been telling her that her family was trying to kill her, she would want to think it through first before reacting. She would need to be totally sure.

"Listen, I gotta prepare for a call in a little bit. After the call, I'll be back over here. But I need you to take this, just in case."

Keisha looked down at Trigga's outstretched hand and her mouth fell wide open. Shaking her head vigorously, she pushed the object away from her.

"No, I can't take that," she said as she continued to shake her head at him. "The last time I held a gun…I can't. I'll be fine."

"Either you take this or you come with me. Those are your options. I need to make sure you're safe. You're in this shit because of me," Trigga told her firmly as he pushed it towards her again.

The way that he looked at her let her know that he wasn't going to take her refusal as an option. Keisha nodded her head, swallowed hard and then held out her hand for the gun. Before giving it to her, Trigga held it up and pointed at it.

"Click this button to turn off the safety before pulling the trigger. There is already one in the chamber. All you have to do is turn off the safety, then aim and shoot. Got it?" he asked her with a raised brow.

Keisha nodded her head. When Trigga handed her the gun, she held it awkwardly in her hand, unsure of exactly where to put it. After giving him an uneasy look, to which he responded with a wink, she jumped out of his ride and decided to just hide the weapon under her shirt and make a mad dash to the door.

As soon as Keisha ran in her room, she placed the gun in the drawer of her nightstand along with the other items she had stashed there, including over a dozen sandwich bags full of coke, pills and several thousands of dollars she had taken from Lloyd the day she barely escaped with her life.

For some reason, she just stared at all the paraphernalia and suddenly she felt a timorous shiver rise up her spine, as she dove onto her bed with tears in her eyes. She hated that she was being such a crybaby but at the moment, she felt like she had so much stress on her and there was nothing she could do about it and no one she could run to. She just wanted to rewind her life to a point where it was normal and stay in that moment.

Now she was holding drugs and caught up in a situation that she knew nothing about. Lloyd and Trigga's brother, Mase, would kill her if they found her, and she didn't have the faintest idea what to do about that or where to go. She had no family or friends outside of Atlanta. She could take the money she took from Lloyd and go but to where? And how long would the money last?

Halfway into her pity-party, Keisha's phone chimed. Wiping at the tears that were rolling down her cheeks, Keisha grabbed it and stared at the screen. In true Trigga-fashion, he'd read her mind and was there to put it at ease.

You'll be fine. I got you, he'd texted her.

Keisha smiled through her tears and wiped her face.

Thank you, she texted him back feeling a ray of hope that only came from the protection of a man.

Two seconds later he responded.

You're welcome. Now stop all that damn crying and close the blinds in your room. Your nosey ass roommate left them open.

Frowning, Keisha's eyes shot up to her window and she saw that she was looking directly into Trigga's front windshield. Although she couldn't see him, he had a perfect line of vision to her. He'd seen her mini-breakdown and all. No wonder he knew what to text.

"TIIISSSSHHH!" Keisha yelled out as she closed the blinds. She could just imagine Trigga laughing at her from behind his tint. "BRING YOUR NOSEY ASS HERE!"

THREE

"Man, nigga, what you mean?" Mase fumed through the phone. "So you not gone be able to make the call?"

"Naw, we can do the call, I'm just not at the room," Trigga told him as he sat in the middle of a small coffee shop in Buckhead. He was trying to talk low but even still he saw a few of the patrons casting annoyed glances at him.

"Well, how we gone do it? Three-way or some shit?" Mase asked.

"Yeah, that'll work. Queen will call me and I'll add you on the line," Trigga told him. "I'm not gonna be at the room until later on but she wanna have the call in about thirty minutes." Trigga checked his watch out of habit although he already knew what time it was.

He was feeling antsy for some reason. He also was feeling like he was being watched. Lifting his head, he scanned the coffee shop for a minute as he half-listened to Mase talk about how his funds were low and he needed the job. Then his eyes fell upon the gentle stare of a woman sitting diagonal to him. She had milk chocolate skin that seemed to glow. Her hair was pulled neatly into a ponytail, exposing her long, elegant neck and toned arms. As soon as his stare met hers, she blushed and turned away from him. Trigga found that funny and made a short, snorting noise as he watched her pretend to read a flyer on her table.

"We takin' the job as soon as we get this current job finished with. She gettin' mad as fuck that the shit takin' so long. Only reason she gave us this long is because she got her hands full with some other shit," Trigga responded to Mase.

A server came over to ask him if he wanted another coffee or anything else. She made sure to put extra emphasis on the 'anything else' that she was offering. Trigga mouthed 'no' to her and then tuned back into his conversation with Mase. His eyes fell upon the woman across from him and he noticed that she was studying him once again. Throwing her a small smile, he waved and she sent him a bashful wave back.

"A'ight, well, I'll be waitin' on the line for the call," Mase said.

"Bet," Trigga responded. "Aye, quick question."

"What's up?"

"The night I went after Lloyd at the club and them niggas set me up, where the fuck were you?"

An older woman dramatically gasped at Trigga's language, bringing her hand to her chest and then frowned. He shot her an annoyed look and then turned away from her as he waited for Mase to respond.

"I was chillin' wit' some chicks from the club. Yo', I felt like shit about that night. I ain't even know that you was goin' to be goin' after that nigga like that. And you usually got that shit handled so…Man, my bad," Mase said to him.

Although he was trying to sound sincere, his face was blank and emotionless. He couldn't wait until he was able to put a bullet through Trigga's skull so he could be done playing this lil' game.

"Yo, something else had been troubling me that night at the club. You was actin' strange and unconcerned like you really wasn't feelin' murkin' dude and his crew."

Trigga clinched his jaw as he pondered his thoughts carefully. If Keisha was telling the truth and his brother was trying to kill him, he couldn't let him know he was on to it.

"Naw'll, I wasn't in any hurry to clap them niggaz 'cause shit was lookin' lovely. Them niggaz was like prey on an ordinary day. You know how we rock! Lullaby they bitch asses to sleep, then BAM! Pounce on dat ass! Besides, I was tryin' to get my dick wet with them fine ass ATL bitches and murk them niggaz later on a smooth creep…like how we normally rock, na'mean?"

Silence.

Trigga held the phone so tight his knuckles paled white as he thought. All the while, the turbulent ebb and flow of his emotions were centered around the implications of what would happen if it turned out what Keisha said was really true?

Could she be lying?

Hopefully his brother wasn't. But it seemed to him that Mase was trying too hard to make it seem like he wasn't on some crazy shit that night at the club.

"Nigga, you still on the phone?" Mase asked with an attitude, raising his voice.

"Yeah, yeah," Trigga responded as he contemplated his thoughts carefully and moistened his lips with a dry tongue. It felt like he was about to have an anxiety attack. Ever since they were little boys, he had always known how to catch his brother in a lie. Mentally, he prepared to set the trap.

"Tell me something, Mase."

"What, nigga? And make it quick. I found an online website where bitches selling pussy."

"Tell me, how did you know I was at the hospital, and how did you know to move the car that was shot up when they ambushed us?" Trigga asked and for some reason he couldn't help closing his eyes tightly as he suddenly felt the throb of his temple pulsating.

"I...I... uhh, umm, I saw that shit on the news or some shit," Mase stuttered.

"Nigga, you just told me you stayed at the club that night tryna fuck some bitches!" Trigga barked as he suddenly stood up.

Several patrons were now watching him, including the attractive chick at the table. Trigga didn't care, his blood was boiling and he was fuming mad.

"Nigga, what's up with da hundred questions? I'm yo' fuckin' brother, your fuckin' blood! We fam! What's going on? Is there something you want to talk to me about? If you can't trust yo' fuckin' own twin brother, who da fuck can you trust?"

"I was thinking the same thing," Trigga said in somber tone. As he thought on Mase's words, he happened to glance at his mired reflection in the glass window. Again, he noticed the female staring at him intensely.

What the fuck is up with her? he thought.

Mase gave his brother a dry cackle when he said, "Chill man, you always on some paranoid shit ever since we were shorties. Let's meet up, burn a coupla blunts, get faded and plot on these slow ass ATL niggaz."

The whole while Mase spoke, he was caressing the blue steel pearl white handle of the nineteen shot Glock .9 mm that he intended to shoot Trigga in his dome with.

"Lemme get my thoughts together," was all Trigga said in a strained voice.

He knew his brother was lying and his heart was heavy at the thought of what he would have to do. Their dear mother would never forgive him for that. Truth be told, nor would his conscious but their deadly confrontation was inevitable and the thought irritated him.

"Fuck!!!!!" Trigga cursed out loud then kicked at the leg of his table in frustration.

When he looked up, the restaurant security officer was approaching him and in his hand was a gun.

"What's yo' muhfuckin' problem? Keep this shit up and I'mma kick yo' long skinny ass outta here!"

Trigga gritted his teeth together and shot a menacing look at the man, as he stood tall in front of him. Just then, a waitress hurried back over with a tray teetering in her hands full of food and drinks.

"Elmo, everything's good." She smiled sweetly at Trigga as she sat the food down at a table next to him and smoothed her apron down over her breast and midriff with the palms of her hands.

Trigga ignored the waitress as he stood up over the security guard and scowled down at him.

"Who da fuck is you? A rent-a-cop or some shit? Get tha fuck, outta here!" Trigga grumbled.

A ripple of laughter erupted in the restaurant causing the security guard's face to flush red. His mouth moved with no words coming out as he fumbled with his gun holster. He couldn't get it out fast enough.

"Fuck you callin' a rent-a-cop? I'll lock your long neck ass up!"

"Come on y'all, stop it!" the waitress said with a pained expression. She'd already had a long day and didn't want to deal with any more bullshit.

"You ain't gone fuck with me! This is a restaurant, I'mma drink my damn coffee and you better get the fuck outta my face with dat bullshit."

"I'mma get the fuck outta your face alright!" the security guard mimicked him, as he continued to fumble with his holster. Finally, he pulled the gun out and held it at his side. "Now, I'mma ask you to leave the premises."

Things had suddenly turned serious as several of the patrons got up and headed for the door. Just then somebody walked up and grabbed Trigga by the arm. Instantly, he pulled away.

"Fuck wrong wit—"

Just as he was about to take off swinging, he realized it was the attractive chick that had been watching him. Up close, she was even more beautiful with long, black, kinky hair shimmering in a frosty blue holder and cascading over her left shoulder in a curly, natural poof. She had a piercing in her right eyebrow and bottom lip. Her complexion was swarthy black like rich dark coffee. Trigga couldn't help but notice her audacious shapely curves in the tight-fitting leggings with ass for days. She wore a pink wife beater with a matching bra underneath. Her ample, double-D breasts stood out like trophies to be admired.

"Don't let him get under your skin. Come on, walk away. Too many of our innocent black men have been getting gunned down lately. Please?" she said. Her mellow tone was persuasive, as she looked at him with angelic hazel eyes and then placed a hand on his shoulder. She tried to smile but only her eyes twinkled with an amber glow that hinted at urgency.

"Yea, you better get his ass outta here before I bust a cap in his long, skinny ass," the security guard threatened and began to bounce on the balls of his feet with excitement and newfound confidence.

"Yo nigga, what's going on? Trigga, what's going on?" The voice belonged to Mase. Trigga had forgot all about him still being on the phone until his voice thundered through Trigga's earpiece.

"I'mma holla at'cha later," Trigga said while still staring at the security guard.

"Meet you at—" Before Mase could finish the statement, Trigga disconnected the call.

"Walk away." The young woman tugged at his arm and pulled him out of his trance. He suddenly came back to his senses then shrugged the female's hand off him and walked towards the door.

"Hey, who is going to pay for your drink?" the waitress said.

Without turning around, Trigga jabbed a finger towards the security guard still standing by his table.

"He is."

FOUR

An ardent bright sun set high in the sky, embellished by sublime blue skies as Trigga stalked out the restaurant deep in his thoughts. He was in foreign city, in a distant land with the thought of murder weighing on him heavily…the murder of his own flesh and blood, his beloved brother.

Suddenly, he heard the chime of a door opening behind him followed by the sound of footsteps coming up behind him. There was no doubt it was the whack-ass security guard determined to continue their confrontation on the street. Pissed off to the fullest, Trigga acted on instincts and survival mode. With the quickness, as people passed on the crowded street, he reached in his waist and came up with his banger in one swift motion. Midway, he stopped when he realized his blunder and tried to hide his weapon.

Too late!

The startled expression on her face said it all, as her delicate eyebrows rose with a hint fear. She stopped in her tracks and clasped a hand over her right breast. Furtively, he stashed his banger in the back of his pants. So much had been going on, things had been moving so fast and he wasn't on his shit, with everything concerning

Mase swirling around his mind. But the last thing he wanted was to frighten a stranger that wasn't involved in his mix.

"Damn shawty, I apologize," he said with a shrug as he observed her.

Her thick hair blew in the wind. She wiped a lock of hair from her forehead as she expelled a deep breath. For some reason she didn't look at him as sunlight glistened off her eyes. Unsure of how to handle the awkward moment, Trigga swiveled on his feet to walk away.

"I was just trying to look out for you…from the moment you walked into the restaurant I couldn't help thinking you look like…like…somebody I used to know," she said quietly as is if heavy in her thoughts.

"Things did get out of hand. I apologize. But naw, you don't know me," he said. He continued to walk away but he heard her steps behind him.

"Well, what's your name?" she asked.

Trigga groaned inwardly and closed his eyes. He didn't have time for any of this shit. It seemed like the more he tried to get away from women, the more they showed up and wouldn't go away. Although he felt something for Keisha, part of him wished that she hadn't followed him that night at the club. Then he wouldn't be worried about her in addition to whatever was going on with Mase.

"You can call me…Jamel," he answered as he turned around. He wasn't comfortable with giving her his real name or his nickname because, no matter how beautiful and innocent she seemed, she was someone he didn't know.

She stared at him without saying anything, which intensified the awkward feeling he was already feeling. He extended his hand to her, which seemed unnatural to him but he did it anyways in an effort to appear kind.

"NeTasha. But you can call me Tasha," she responded. She grabbed his hand and held it a second too long. Trigga noted it, but waited until she pulled away.

"Well, it was nice meeting you," Trigga said and began to walk away again.

"Ohhh, you running now?" Tasha chided him.

"Running?" he quipped, making a face as he stopped in his tracks and turned to her. Something about his behavior made her smile.

"Yes, we are just getting acquainted and all I know about you is that your name is Jamel and that you have a sexy accent. Then you try to run off," she said while placing her hand on her hip. For some reason the small gesture made him smile; it also aroused his manhood.

He couldn't help it and gave her body a quick once over. She caught him looking and blushed. Remembering that he had enough shit already on his plate to deal with, he tore his eyes away from her, more determined than before to keep it moving.

For a nigga who is normally focused on business, you seem to have issues gettin' rid of these chicks that keep popping up, he thought to himself.

"I have a lot going on. Today has been one of them days. You don't have a clue."

"Oh, yes I do," Tasha told him. "You almost got shot by that Smurf looking security guard."

They both laughed. Then Trigga glanced at his watch and frowned. She read his demeanor.

"At least walk me to the bus stop. Then you can leave, I promise," she said sweetly as she beamed with a smile. It took everything in his power not to offer her a ride. But, remembering what happened the last time he offered a fine ass female a ride, he nodded and they took off walking.

"Where you headed?" he asked while guiding her across the street by her elbow in all the heavy traffic and crowd around them.

"Gotta get to the Marta station. I go to Clark Atlanta. I'm studying criminal justice. I want to be a lawyer," she answered looking up at him.

"Oh, your ass is a brainiac. You've probably been studying me the whole time like Gideon law."

Tasha nearly stumbled as she walked looking up at him. Bemused she asked, "What you know about Gideon Law?

"It's a landmark case. The right to counsel." He made an expression like that was something everyone should know.

"You're smart, too," Tasha said looking at him in admiration.

"I went to college on a basketball scholarship."

"What happened?" she inquired and stopped walking as if she expected a long explanation.

"What you mean what happened?" He was slightly offended like she was implying there was something wrong with him. He continued, "I'm good Ma, ain't hurtin' for nothin'. I just decided to take a different route."

She frowned making a face like she wasn't buying it.

"Okay, I had a sports injury and couldn't play ball, then my mama was having financial problems so I had to get it from the muscle."

"So basically you dropped out of college and started hustling?" she summarized his statement.

"I plead the fifth," he retorted smartly, throwing up the palms of his hand. Tasha couldn't help but notice the iced out Rolex watch glimmering on his wrist.

Then it happened out of the blue as they passed a soul food restaurant, where two homeless people stood outside begging for money. They were both filthy dirty and disheveled. The stench of their bodies you could smell a mile away.

"Boy, how you doing?" the homeless man asked then scratched at his privates like something down there was biting him with razor teeth.

Trigga damn near vomited and, to make matters worse, the hot humid breeze was pushing the funk right in his face. He glanced over at Tasha and she was wrinkling up her nose, with a look as if she was holding her breath but didn't want to be obvious about it. She tried to play it off by smiling.

The homeless man scratched again, then called over to his companion. She was deep into a heavy argument with herself. She ambled over to him as Trigga started to walk away.

"Don't you remember him?" he asked her.

"Yea, sure do," she replied then added, "What ever happened to that girl? Did she make it? Is she still alive?" the homeless woman asked with sincere compassion.

Then it hit Trigga like a ton of bricks and he stopped dead in his tracks. It was the homeless couple that helped them find the hospital on the dark and dreary night Keisha and he had been ambushed, badly bleeding and shot multiple times. If it had not been for them, Trigga and Keisha could have very well died.

"Yea, she's good. Thank y'all so much," Trigga said instantly overwhelmed with guilt, as people walked by giving the homeless couple disgusting looks of disdain. He reached into his pocket to give them some money and realized Tasha had already beaten him to it. She passed each one of them a few crumpled one-dollar bills.

Trigga pulled out a large wad of money and peeled off a few hundred-dollar bills to add to hers. Tasha's eyes got big as saucers as she watched him give the homeless people the money. Tacitly, she smiled and nodded her approval.

"Thank you! Thank you!" Both of the homeless people erupted in chorus and began to do some type of happy dance in the middle of the sidewalk as people scurried by them.

"I want you all to take that money, get a room and buy some clothes and food."

Suddenly the homeless man stopped dancing and furrowed his brow.

"How I'mma get a room for me and my wife? We homeless, we don't have no identification, no nothing," he said with grim expression.

Trigga glanced over at Tasha and she gave him a quizzical shrug, like 'what do we do next?' Trigga had a remedy for that. He truly intended to bless the homeless people for saving him and Keisha's life. He wanted to give them a night they would never forget. He pulled them to the side and passed them a key then gave them instructions. The looks on their faces were as if they had won the lottery.

Then as the homeless couple rushed off Trigga shouted, "Don't forget to take full advantage of the showers and bathtub."

Tasha swatted his arm, "Don't be so cruel!" She laughed as he shrugged at her.

"Never that, but you have to admit they both were a little musky," Trigga joked with a grin.

"No, what I have to admit is that was generous of you giving them all that money. Where do you know them from?"

He glanced at his wrist again and lied with a straight face. "A friend and I were in a car accident and those two homeless people just happened to stumble upon us. They saved our lives. We needed directions to get to the hospital and they went out of their way to get us there or else my friend could have died."

"Oh… a friend? By any chance does your friend happen to be your girlfriend?"

He stopped for a second and looked squarely at Tasha. "No."

Just then his iPhone chimed. He checked the caller ID and it was Keisha. Trigga felt a strange feeling wash over him. It was almost like she knew he was thinking about her. He threw up a finger as if to say 'wait a sec' to Tasha and stepped away.

"Yo, what's good?" he spoke into the phone.

"You. I was just checking on you. Is everything okay? I … I do want to see you again…soon," she said in a timid voice.

A small smile crept up in the corner of Trigga's face as he listened to her. It wasn't every day that Keisha used this kind of tone that made her sound vulnerable. Her texts were always short and whenever he called to check in with her in the past, she tried to act like she was holding everything down with ease, although he knew she was faking it.

"Yea, I want to see you too. But I got to handle some situations," he said thinking about the difficult task at hand with his brother. As much as he wanted to pretend that the issue with his brother didn't exist, he couldn't.

The whole while as he talked, Tasha was looking at him closely like she was reading his lips.

"I know and I'm scared," Keisha pouted over the phone. The sound of her voice tugged at his heartstrings. He glanced at Tasha and noticed her examining his face but didn't think much of it as he continued speaking to Keisha.

"Don't be. You're good. I left you with some heat and I even showed you how to use it. Okay?" he reminded her, trying to instill confidence in her.

"But the last time I had a gun…I'm just…I'm scared," she complained and he sighed. He had too much going on and this additional shit wasn't helping it.

Trigga mopped at his forehead in frustration. He looked up and saw that Tasha had an expression on her face like she had bit into a sour lemon as she watched him intensely.

"Okay, let me think," he muttered, flustered, into the phone.

Something panged deep in his chest. He wondered if he was catching too many feelings for her. They had been through so much in a short span of time. As much as he hated to admit it, it had all been partially his fault. They both were emotionally and physically bonded to each other because of their experiences.

But still in the dark crevice of his mind, in that place that was often sacred and sheltered when it came to family and loved ones, there was a dualism as he tried to figure out whether to be logical or emotional. He prayed his logic was telling him right about his brother and even more so that he was making the right decision with Keisha by allowing himself to catch feelings for her.

As much as he hated to admit it, she was trampling all over his 'Money Over Bitches' rule. In fact, she had become his emotional soft spot, if a gangsta ever had one. He was in violation of his thug's code of ethics.

"Okay…I'm going to pick you later on tonight and take you away from there so you can get your mind off everything. Stop worrying."

"Can we finish off where we left off with our date?" Keisha asked him. For the first time since the call, she started to sound hopeful and excited.

There was something so titillating and captivating about the sound of her voice, it caused him to smirk with a pixilated grin. He completely forgot Tasha was there as he focused his attention on Keisha.

Trigga just stared out in space as he thought about the soft contours of her thighs, her sensuous hips and her luscious conical breasts, which were the size of ripe cantaloupe. He could see himself tearing her clothes off and then throwing her panties and bra along with the rest of their clothes throughout the residence.

"Humph! Really?" An intrusive voice interrupted his thoughts, throwing him out of his reverie.

"Oh, yea …my bad, Ma," he replied with a shrug and frown, as he scrutinized Tasha standing in front of him with attitude all over her face. He wanted to ask her what the fuck she was mad about. She wasn't his chick.

"Was that a female voice I heard? Are you with a girl?" Keisha questioned in his ear.

"Uhhh, no. I mean yeah, sort of. It ain't nobody."

NeTasha gave him an icy look and scribbled her number on a piece of paper, shoved it in his pocket and took off into a trot for the bus. He couldn't help but admire her round backside as it bounced from side-to-side.

"Who is she?" Keisha continued.

"Nobody, just some chick asking for directions. She's gone and on the bus now." Trigga tactfully changed the subject.

He watched NeTasha board her bus. She frowned and gestured, pointing at his phone, and mouthed, "That's your girlfriend." Trigga caught her message and smiled to himself as the bus passed him by.

"I'll come get you later on and we'll finish our date."

"What about your brother?" Keisha asked tersely, not bothering to hide her apprehension.

"Don't worry yo' lil' ass 'bout that. When I say I got it, I got it," Trigga said assumingly and possibly underestimating the situation. "Let me hit you back later."

Trigga hung up the phone before she could respond. He had a job to do and not long to do it.

***

Keisha hung up the phone and sat it on her nightstand, as she wiped the tears from her eyes and sat down on her bed. She pulled out her Physics book and tried to concentrate on the lesson for the day. She wasn't in class because, to be honest, she couldn't stomach a lecture that day. Her mind was on Trigga, Lloyd, Mase and the gun sitting in the drawer of her nightstand.

The last time she'd held a gun, she'd almost ruined a life when she'd nearly killed Lloyd and his pregnant wife. It was a day that she didn't want to remember so she'd tried to wipe it from her mind. Now she had the gun Trigga had given her, which was a constant reminder not only of that day, but also the dangerous situation that she'd found herself in.

Grabbing the phone again, she dialed a number and held on the line while the phone rang. When the line answered, Keisha heard a lot of noise in the background before the person on the other line finally answered.

"Hello?"

"Hey girl, this Keesh. I was wondering if I could borrow your notes from class. I'm sorry to ask but I'm having the hardest time right now."

"Don't mention it, Keesh. I'll email it to you…er, let me call you back later, okay? I can barely hear you."

"Okay. Thank you so much!" Keisha hung up the phone and turned back towards the book on her bed. But less than two seconds later, she was back to daydreaming about other things, mainly Trigga's sexy ass.

Pulling herself from out of her daydream, Keisha looked up when she heard three light taps on her door. It was Tish.

"Hey," Tish said. She had a worried expression on her face.

"Hey," Keisha responded. She wiped again at her face and tried to smile but from the look on Tish's face, she could see that her forced smile did nothing to hide her mood.

"I'm about to head out to the club and try to get some extra hours in. You gonna be alright here by yourself?"

Keisha wanted to say no, but she nodded her head anyways. "Yeah, I'm hoping that Trigga will be here soon, anyways."

Tish gave her a look and then walked in the room and sat down on the bed. "You think that's best? I mean…ever since I've known you, you've been caught up in some shit with him. Maybe some distance is what you need."

Keisha gave her a look and snorted. "I'm surprised you would say that from the way your mouth was hanging wide open when he came over here."

Tish smiled and ran her hand through her hair. "Well, the nigga is *fine* but I heard the conversation you just had with him and I see how you're looking right now. You have a good future ahead of you and being pulled in some gangster shit that ain't even 'bout you…that's not a good look."

Keisha nodded her head. "I know." She sighed and closed her eyes for a minute as she thought about what Tish was saying. Then she opened her eyes and looked into her friend's caring eyes.

"You're right. I'll talk to him about everything when he picks me up tonight. And I'll give him back his gun."

Tish sighed and stood up. "Well, I'on know about all *that*. We can use some protection in here. We do live in the muthafuckin' hood," she laughed and Keisha joined in, despite her feelings.

"We can keep that but I can look at you and tell that you ain't no ride or die type bitch, Keesh. You're more of a 'ride and live comfy' bitch. This thug shit ain't in you."

Keisha sat quietly and thought about Tish's words as she walked out of the room. She was right. The entire ordeal was stressing her the fuck out and it was taking everything in her power not to pull out a bag of the coke that she'd stole from Lloyd's spot and snort her worries away.

FIVE

Trigga knew he was dead ass wrong but he couldn't stop himself. At the same time, he reasoned that he wasn't in the wrong. Keisha wasn't his girlfriend so he didn't have any loyalties to her. Although he felt in himself that he did, the fact of the matter was that she was just some chick he knew. She'd gotten herself mixed up in his shit and he felt bad about that so he also felt the need to protect her, but she wasn't *his* girl. Therefore, what he chose to do with his dick and the tight, sweet pussy in front of him was his business.

"Jamel, I've never done this before," Tasha whispered as she looked at him. Trigga frowned slightly then he remembered that Jamel was the name he had given her and relaxed.

Tasha was butt-naked, like the day she was born. Trigga licked his lips and looked at her sexy ass, ignoring what she was saying. He didn't care whether or not she'd done this before or not. He needed some pussy…no strings attached type pussy. He didn't want to get up and have feelings.

It was why he chose to fuck Tasha before he went to see Keisha. If he let himself do something wit Keisha that night, he was afraid that he wouldn't be able to get her out of his mind. At the moment, he hadn't even done anything with her and she had a nigga fiending for her presence as it was. What the hell would happen if he did fuck her and her pussy was everything he thought it was?

After he hung up the phone with Keisha, he hopped in the whip and drove over to the East side where he knew Lloyd's thugs ran free. He was able to catch up with two of the top niggas in Lloyd's crew, Grimey and Murder, who had been with him at the club that infamous night. Trigga knew Lloyd would be home soon and he wanted to send a message to him before he even got back on the streets. Queen had given him a list of niggas to take care of in addition to Lloyd.

"Kenyon, AK, Murder, Grimey and Roach…" Trigga muttered under his breath.

In a dark black Impala that he'd rented that morning, Trigga sat outside the stash spot that he'd located the day before he first saw Keisha and waited. After about fifteen minutes of sitting and counting the bodies, he noted it was about fifteen niggas inside, more than he could handle on his own, and he couldn't see faces. Then a skinny, bowlegged man walked outside. While yapping on his phone, he bent the corner to take a piss. Shaking his head, Trigga chuckled lightly to himself, jumped out the whip and walked right up on him.

When he got to him, he pressed his gun against the man's skull right as he hung up his phone and began pulling up his pants. The man jumped and stopped moving immediately.

"Fuckin' move and I'll put a bullet in ya' bitch ass. Walk wit' me," he commanded the man.

One thing was for certain, the man seemed to be a straight gangsta through and through. He didn't bat an eye when Trigga walked up on him. He simply placed his hands to his side and moved with Trigga behind the house next door.

"Who da fuck all in there?" Trigga asked once they stopped walking.

"Nigga, I'm EPG. I'm ready to die fo' dis shit!" the man snarled at him, his back still to Trigga and the cold barrel of the gun pressed against his head. Snickering, Trigga clicked his tongue and pulled the gun away. Then he quickly fired off a shot in the man's foot.

"AHHH—" his screams were cut off by Trigga slamming the butt of the gun hard against his head.

"Who in there?" he repeated. "Yell and I'mma shoot ya in ya other foot." The man's bottom lip quivered and his face was twisted up from the pain he felt. He started teetering forward as if the pain was making his right leg go limp.

When he didn't answer immediately, Trigga pointed the gun to his foot.

"WAIT! SHIT! It's EP, Tony, Grimey, Cali, and Roach. Damn!"

Two outta the five…

"And what's yo' name?"

"June Bug!" he winced, and slowly bent his neck down to look at his bloody foot. His eyes bugged when he saw that his shoe was totally soaked with the blood, almost to the point that you couldn't see anything else.

"Gimme your cell phone," Trigga told him. The man reached down and pulled his cell out of his pocket with a shaky hand. Trigga snatched it from him and started scrolling through his contacts.

Yo' man, I—"

Trigga let off a shot in the man's head and his body fell like a sack of potatoes onto the wet grass. He sent a text to Grimey.

Black on da phone. Wanna talk to u n Roach outside. I'm out back.

Trigga crept out from behind the house next door and waited for the two gangsters to walk outside. Grimey was the first one to bend the corner and he was the recipient of the first bullet that came from Trigga's gun. Stepping out from behind the house, he caught Roach in the back of the head. Before he hopped in his whip to leave, he grabbed Grimey and Roach's cells and sent a text to the numbers saved for AK and Murder.

TQC was all it said and was all it needed to say. He knew that they would spread the word to Lloyd and Kenyon that The Queen Cartel had struck again.

After taking care of business, Trigga couldn't even lie. He had pussy on his mind. He needed to relax, clear his mind and regroup. So, he called the number he had for Tasha. She already knew the deal with Keisha from the conversation she'd overheard earlier and from the way she had thrown herself at him, he thought she would be more than ready.

Trigga's mind was all over the place and he was stressed like a muthafucka. Nothing like some good pussy to help put his mind at ease and, just as he thought, when he called Tasha, she was at home and readily invited him over. And that's how he landed himself here...in her room, licking his lips as he admired her sexy, curvy body, and smooth mocha-colored skin.

"Mmmm, that feels so good," Tasha moaned as Trigga stirred the inside of her pussy with his two fingers. The smacking noise it was making as he did it let him know that she was wet...just what he needed.

Test one passed, he thought to himself.

Then he pulled his fingers out and, in a real slick undercover way, passed his fingers quickly in front of his nose so that he could get a whiff of her sex. She smelled like fresh pussy with a hint of Jasmine from whatever body wash or lotion she used.

She's clean. Test two passed.

Pulling up, Trigga pulled a condom down on his dick and then pushed her legs wide open gently. He leaned down and pulled in one of her chocolate drop nipples into his mouth and sucked hard. Tasha gasped out loud and her legs opened wider, as she prepared for him to enter her. And that's just what he did.

"OW!" Tasha yelped out once he entered in. Trigga stopped moving suddenly.

"You okay?" he asked as he looked in her pain-filled eyes.

"Yeah, I'm good. You're so…big. Can you just go a little slower?"

Trigga nodded his head but he was a little frustrated. He didn't want to go slow. He just wanted to fuck so he could get a nut and clear his mind. This slow, lovemaking shit wasn't a part of his plans. Sighing, he slowed it down and pulled out a little so that he wasn't all the way in.

Tasha let out a soft, long moan as he stroked gently in her, and Trigga gripped the sheets tightly while biting his bottom lip. It had been so long since he'd had sex because of all the shit going on so that, combined with the fact that Tasha was tight as hell, had him damn near forcing himself not to cum too fast. Even through the condom, he could feel her velvety cave. She was tight, almost like she was a damn virgin.

"Damn, girl you got some good pussy," he moaned into her ear.

"Mmmm! God, this is starting to feel so good," she said through her teeth as she slowly began grinding against him.

Trigga leaned up and looked at her face; her eyes were tightly closed and she was biting down on her bottom lip as she twerked awkwardly against him. As he stroked slowly, he continued to watch her. She was beautiful but still he wished she were Keisha.

Shit, I'm trippin', he thought to himself. Here he was in some of the best pussy he'd had in his life and he was thinking about another woman.

Closing his eyes, Trigga continued pushing in and out of Tasha but he still couldn't get the image of Keisha out of his mind. When he opened his eyes and he saw Tasha instead of her, he felt his erection going down.

Shit!

"Is everything alright?" Tasha asked him.

"Yeah, it's all good," he lied. He pulled out and started stroking his dick. When he looked into Tasha's eyes, he saw that she was giving him a concerned look.

"You don't...I don't feel good to you?" she asked him. The expression on her face made him feel like shit.

"Yeah, Ma," he said. "Actually, you almost feel too good. A nigga tryin' to keep from bustin' quickly, that's all." That made her smile. "Turn over," he said.

Tasha wasted no time turning over and lifting her ass high up in the air. Trigga smiled and smacked it hard as he pulled up on top of her. Pushing himself in, he stirred around in her and closed his eyes and thought of Keisha. His dick got rock hard and he started fucking the shit out of Tasha's pussy, with the vision of Keisha's sweet face in his mind's eye. When he opened his eyes, the back of Tasha's head allowed him to continue imagining that it was Keisha and not Tasha who was moaning and yelling out his name, as he continued to fuck her like she had the best pussy in the world.

"Shit, Keesh! Got damn!" he yelled out right as he was about to come. Not realizing his blunder, he continued stroking and pushing up into Tasha's pussy until he felt the orgasm rise up through his dick. He was so lost in ecstasy and thoughts of Keisha that he didn't even realize that Tasha had gone rigid and her moaning had stopped.

"Damn, you got some good shit. Fuck," Trigga said once he pulled out of her.

Tasha flipped around and pulled away from him slowly. She had an odd look in her eyes but Trigga couldn't tell why, so he dismissed it and got up to walk to the bathroom. When he turned on the light, he looked down to remove the condom but was caught off guard by something he saw.

"Shit…you on your period?" he yelled from inside the bathroom. When Tasha didn't answer, he poked his head out to look at her. "Hello?"

Tasha had her head down. When she raised it up to look at him, he saw that she had tears in her eyes. "No."

"Well, there is blood on the condom," he said to her as he pointed to the rubber still on his dick. "What the fuck you cryin' for?"

Tasha sniffled and wiped the tears from her eyes. "I told you…I never done this before."

Dread overcame Trigga as the realization of what she'd meant came over him. He'd thought she was saying she'd never slept with a nigga on the first night before; that's what all the bitches he'd fucked as soon as he met them had said. But she'd meant that she had never had sex before. She was a damn virgin.

"FUCK!" Trigga shouted out as he rubbed his hand over his face. The smell of Tasha's dried pussy juices on his finger stung his nose. "Man, Tasha…I'm sorry. I didn't know that's what you meant."

"You said her name when you came," she responded quietly.

"What?" Trigga asked her, only half-listening as he tried to take the condom off without touching any of the blood. Finally he snatched it off and tossed it down the toilet bowl before flushing it.

How could I be so damn stupid? he thought.

Messing with virgins was bad news. He had a lot of shit already weighing on his conscience and he didn't want to have this on there, too. It was bad enough that he was planning on fucking and leaving. Now he found out that she had probably been saving her virginity for Jesus, and he'd messed up what should have been a good experience between her and some lame, goofy ass college nigga.

"When you came…you said 'Keesh'. You said her name…" Tasha's voice trailed off.

Trigga looked up at her and saw that she was wiping tears from her eyes.

I can't deal with this shit right now, he thought.

"Tasha, look, I'm sorry. I didn't think you were a virgin." He paused as he tried to find the right words to fix the situation so he could get the hell out of there. "Technically, you still a virgin, if you think about it. I didn't put my whole dick in there. So you good."

Tasha looked at him like she wasn't convinced. Trigga sighed and started pulling on his clothes. There was nothing else he could do. He damn sure wasn't about to be her boyfriend or nothin'.

"Listen, I'll leave you my number. Call me if you need anything," he said. "I have to go handle some shit that I forgot about and I'll catch up with you later."

After getting dressed, he scribbled his number down on a sheet of paper and handed it to Tasha. The whole time before he walked out of her front door, he tried to ignore the look of longing, sadness and hurt in her eyes.

SIX

Keisha heard the sound of the engine of Trigga's Porsche truck as soon as he pulled up outside her apartment, and her heart started beating quickly with the anticipation she felt. It was a crazy feeling to be so caught up on someone that she didn't really know, but at the same time she enjoyed it.

However, Tish's words weight heavily on her mind. It was true that ever since she'd met him, her life had been spiraling out of control. After getting over Lloyd, she'd only wanted peace and normality but that wasn't what she was getting with Trigga. Things were crazier than ever.

Sitting up on her bed, Keisha pushed her Physics book to the side. She hadn't been reading anything anyways. She was still on the same page that she'd been when she first started. She'd reread that page nearly a dozen times and couldn't remember a thing she'd read. Her mind had been on the man who was now outside her door.

Keisha placed her feet into her light tan and gold Michael Kors slides and walked to the front door. She grabbed her purse from off the table next to the door. She wasn't as dolled up as she had been the first day that she'd gone to Trigga's hotel, but she didn't feel the need to go the extra mile. He'd seen her first thing in the morning so he knew what she looked like. He'd also seen her high out of her mind, so he knew what she looked like at her worst as well.

When Keisha walked up to Trigga's window, she looked him right in the eyes but she could tell that there was something bothering him. If she knew him like she thought she knew him, she knew that he would never tell her the truth about whatever it was. Most likely it had something to do with his brother.

"Hey," was all she said once she sat down on the dark leather seats in his whip.

"Hey yourself," he responded.

A thin smile crossed Keisha's face as Trigga pulled out of the parking lot. So many thoughts were circling in her mind and none of them were on what she'd told Tish that she would tell him. Getting rid of Trigga was the furthest thing from her mind at the moment. The attraction she felt for him was at an all-time high and, even though she still knew that she was in danger, she pushed that from her mind and tried to live in the moment. If this was going to be the last day that she spent with Trigga, she at least wanted it to be a good one before she told him that she wanted out.

"Where are we going?" Keisha asked suddenly as she looked out the window.

"To my room. You said you wanted a repeat of the other night, right?" Trigga said with a flat tone. Something was still bothering him.

"Are you okay?" Keisha asked him.

He turned around and looked at her as if he were seeing her for the first time and then his eyes softened on her face.

"I'm good," he said to her. "Just got some shit on my mind."

I know, Keisha thought to herself.

She felt guilty all of a sudden for asking him for this night. Of course his mind was on something else. If anyone had found out that their brother was trying to kill them, they wouldn't have been able to focus on anything else either.

"I'm sorry about this…why don't you just take me back home?" Keisha asked.

Trigga gave her a look and then sighed. Two seconds later, he had pulled on the side of the road and was looking her directly in her eyes.

"Keesh, you said you wanted me to get you and take you back to my spot so that's what the fuck I'm doin'. Now you say you want to go home…what the fuck do you want?" Trigga said roughly.

Keisha felt tears come to her eyes at his rough way of speaking and attitude. He'd never spoken to her in that way the entire time she'd known him. Seeing the tears in her eyes made him feel like shit.

"I'm sorry, Keesh. But you know the type of shit that I'm dealin' wit'," Trigga started. He sat back and looked straight ahead so he didn't have to continue to see the image of her wiping tears away beside him. "I want to make you happy but at the same time, I got some fucked up shit going on, understand?"

Out of the corner of his eye, he could see her nod. Turning back to her, his eyes fell on her face. She was looking down but she must have felt his stare on her because she peeked up and looked at him through her moist eyes. Trigga felt a stirring in his soul and he reached over and grabbed her by her chin, pulling her gently towards him.

Keisha allowed him to have his way without resistance. She knew what was coming and the anticipation of it made butterflies erupt in her stomach as she closed her eyes and waited. Less than a second later, the next feeling that she felt was Trigga's lips on hers. She returned his kiss and pulled him in even closer. When he flicked his tongue inside of her mouth, she sucked on it softly. She could feel her juices working down under. She craved him and from the way that he explored her mouth with his tongue, she knew he craved her too.

Then suddenly, a familiar smell crept up Trigga's nose and he pulled away quickly, dropping his hand to his side. The smell of Tasha's pussy was still on his fingers. He hadn't had the chance to wash up before speeding over to get Keisha. Looking up, he saw the confused expression on Keisha's face and knew she deserved an explanation.

"I don't want to move too fast," he said sheepishly, hoping that she believed the lie. "Let's at least get to the room first."

So a nigga can get a damn shower, he finished in his mind.

"Okay, baby," Keisha agreed with understanding. Trigga nearly jumped at her saying 'baby' but it was almost as if she hadn't realized she'd said it.

He turned back to the road and Keisha reached out and laid her hand on his thigh. He looked over at her but her head was turned to look out the window as she rubbed back and forth on his leg in a way that he knew was meant to calm him and put him at ease.

It was at that moment that he realized something that he'd been trying to ignore for a while. Whether he had spoken to her about it or not, the evidence was clear. Keisha was no longer just some girl he knew. She was the girl he cared about. She had a special place in his heart and he had a special place in hers. Trigga wasn't sure exactly how the shit worked for normal people, but it seemed to him that Keisha was most definitely his girlfriend.

And as soon as he got back to his place, he was going to clean the scent of the last chick off of him and consummate the relationship that he was positive that he was ready to start with Keisha.

SEVEN

A lone, luminous full moon shined as bright as the morning sun outside, as a layer of dense fog permeated, hovering like gray smoke in the murky, dark night. An occasional car passed with its headlights illuminating through the night with placid white. A dog barked in the distance next to a house; Mase had carefully positioned himself in the adjourning bushes, outside the parking lot of the hotel that Trigga was staying in.

Too much of a coward, Mase couldn't gather enough courage to come at a time when he thought Trigga was awake and would be expecting him. Instead, he decided to 'creep him'; he wanted to sneak in and catch Trigga off-guard so he could shoot him in the back or in his sleep. That way he wouldn't have to look his brother in his eyes when he did what he'd come to do.

He was watching and waiting for the perfect moment to do the inevitable. This would be his renewed version of Cain and Abel. This was the revenge he had been seeking ever since he could remember how to hate his own flesh and blood. The anxiety of it all quickened his heart to beat so fast he had to take in a tiny sip of air to contain his breathing. For some reason he had an erection, as he shifted his bag of goodies from one hand to the other, making the metallic objects inside cling.

A flash of light illuminated from his brother's hotel room window, causing him to squint his eyes to get a better look as the rain pelted his face. For some reason the dog had stopped barking and was now growling, as Mase continued to back up to get a better view of the shadows moving in the window.

Vaguely, Mase could make out the willowy silhouettes of bodies.

Two people?

He stood perplexed. He wasn't prepared to murder two people. Maybe his brother was in the room with one of them pretty thick, stripper bitches, the kind Trigga used to bring back to the crib when they use to share a condo together. It was before his brother kicked him out accusing him of stealing a couple of his girlfriend's panties. So what Mase liked to sniff panties? He had never stolen them. All six pair of panties he found had been in the dirty clothes hamper. One time the chick walked in on him sniffing a pair while rubbing the other against his pelvis. She slugged him so hard that when he came to consciousness, it felt like the blow she hit him with had actually helped one of his severely crooked tooth turn in the right direction.

Mase took another step back just as he thought he saw his brother removing the female's blouse in the shadow of the window. The nigga was about to get him some action. A crooked smile crossed Mase's face but it dropped when he heard the snarling of a vicious dog right behind him. He turned suddenly and his eyes fell upon a big ass Rottweiler.

"Lawd, Jesus... n...n... nice doggy," Mase muttered and felt a drop of piss threatening to spill out into his pants.

Just as the dog leaped for his throat, Mase was able to thrust the heavy duffle bag with the tools at the animal's massive mouth. He took off like a track-star across the parking lot with the dog momentarily dazed but in hot pursuit, barking and biting at his heels. Mase dove on top of a car but not before the dog was able to take a chunk out of his leg.

"Ouuuch! Shit! Fuck!" Mase kicked and thrashed trying to fight off the attack. He reached in the duffle bag and pulled out a gun, then aimed at the dog.

Then things suddenly took a turn for the worse.

An old white security guard, an ex-military veteran still suffering from Post-Traumatic Stress Disorder after serving in Afghanistan in 1979, heard the commotion and came around in an old rickety golf-cart. Seeing Mase with a gun in the air, he sucked in a breath and immediately came up from the hip with an old ancient .45 Colt revolver. He aimed it at Mase just as he had been trained and shot for the assailant's head. He had survived a tour of duty in Afghanistan and damn sure wasn't going to be back on American soil and be murdered.

BOOM! BOOM! BOOM! BOOM!

Miraculously, the bullets barely missed Mase head by a ninth of an inch and, at the same time, frightened the dog off. Mase leaped from the hood of the car and took off running around the building.

"Why you running you coward?!" the security guard exclaimed winded, while reloading the gun.

***

This had to be one of the worse days of his life, Mase was thinking as he watched the last cruiser police car leave the hotel hours after the security guard had attacked him.

The security guard most have filed some type of report, Mase reasoned as he sat hunched down across the street in a rented black Dodge Charger.

The damn dog had bitten a nice-sized chuck out his leg causing Mase to use a piece of his t-shirt to stop the bleeding. But still it hurt like hell and he prayed the dog didn't have rabies. The last thing he needed was to start foaming out the mouth and go crazy.

After watching the last cruiser drive away, Mase hopped out the car with the duffle bag in his hand. He had already changed into a leather jacket and New York fitted cap. He dashed across the street and walked right up and tried the door; of course it was locked. He feigned being disgusted which wasn't hard to do, as he patted his pockets like he was looking for his keycard. Then out of nowhere he heard a familiar sound he would never forget; it was the fuckin' rickety ass golf-cart.

Suddenly, a car came to a stop behind him as the security cart approached. Mase pulled the cap down over his eyes and prayed like a muthafucka the old dude would keep it moving.

He didn't.

"Can I help you?" the security guard asked with his thick, long gnarly eyebrows raised. His skin was pale white as a sheet. He kept his hand on his holster.

"I'm stayin' here," Mase lied with his eyes casted down at the ground. His heart was pounding so fast in his chest it felt like it was going to explode. Then Mase thought of something. He had a banger concealed in the duffle bag.

"What room you stayin' in?" the security guard asked trying to get a good look at Mase's face under the cap. His voice was dry as sandpaper.

"The penthouse," Mase lied, giving the room that Trigga was in.

"I thought I saw you and a pretty girl go up there hours ago? Or was that yesterday?" he pondered and scratched his bald head.

"Yeah, dat was me," Mase lied and shuffled his feet.

Just then a car door slammed. A white man wearing a trench raincoat and a wide brim hat got out a cab and walked up carrying a briefcase.

"Howdy, gentlemen," he said with a nod of his head and proceeded to install his keycard in the door.

He walked in and so did Mase. Through his peripheral, he could see the security guard staring at him, but Mase paid him no attention as long as he would leave him alone. Mase got on the elevator and entered the code to go to the penthouse. It opened right into Trigga's room, but from what Mase had seen earlier, Trigga was having fun in the bedroom, which was clear across the room from the elevator and down the hall. It would allow Mase to come in without being seen or heard.

The elevator doors opened and Mase began to get excited. In the dim of darkness, his heart began to beat faster. As he reached into the bag, there was everything you could ever imagine.

As he groped in the darkness, his foot bumped into something making a loud noise. He stopped and listened as his heartbeat quickened like a small typhoon. There was no doubt in his mind that if his brother, a light sleeper, caught some shadowy figure creeping around in his hotel room, he wouldn't hesitate to blow them to smithereens.

His first mind was telling him to *Stop! Abandon the mission!* But he wouldn't listen; it was a crucial mistake he would regret later.

Then Mase thought he heard something in the darkness. He detected movement and the click of a gun, maybe. He stopped, standing perfectly still. After waiting, all he heard was music, this time clearer. The radio was on V-103, *The Quiet Storm*. Mase continued to creep along the wall.

In mid-stride, Mase stopped; his hand was shaking like a leaf on a tree as he moved the gun to his other hand and reached for his phone. There was a small flashlight built inside of it.

Perfect for the occasion, he reasoned as his heart continued to quake in chest like a small cyclone.

He turned on the small flashlight and it stabbed at the darkness, in a fluorescent glow like he'd seen in them spooky paranormal movies he enjoyed so much where they cut up people…like he was about to do.

A skinny beam of light caught on to something stewed on the floor. It looked like a pair of old crusty woman underwear. Then there were other clothes thrown throughout the suite: Shoes, shirt, a blouse a bra.

He continued to walk. He saw the bedroom door only a few feet away, slightly ajar. His heart beat faster as he opened it and the fetid stench of sex hit him in the face hard. There was Trigga and some female lying on the bed with the covers up almost over their heads. More clothes were strewn across the room.

Gingerly Mase took timid steps; he aimed the gun at the back of his brother's head. He could barely keep his composure. He would shoot Trigga in the head killing him instantly, burn him beyond recognition and take his body to Queen, playing it off as Lloyd's. The chick had to go, too. He couldn't leave any loose ends.

Leaning forward, as an old Whitney Houston song played on the radio, he placed the gun to the back of the head and hesitated.

This is my brother, my own flesh and blood, he thought.

A piece of him felt unsure of what he was about to do. Then he thought about all the times their mom favored Trigga over him and punished him for not being the 'good son'. Everyone favored

Trigga…even that bitch Queen. She would get hers, too. But first, Trigga had to pay.

Pop! Pop!

The gun jerked in his hand as what looked like orange balls of fire exploded from the muzzle. He had a silencer on the end so it barely made a sound, as the bullets embedded themselves in the skull.

Then to Mase's utter shock, the woman in the bed sprung up like a Jack N' the Box. Her face looked old and weary with her hair splayed everywhere on her head, untamed. She began to scream to the top of her lungs. Mase attempted to silence her with the hatchet he had in his other hand. He swung so hard, the sound of the hatchet missing her scalp whistled in the air.

With the adroitness of a young woman, she ducked all three times Mase tried to assault her with the hatchet as she continued to scream what sounded like bloodcurdling shrills. Finally, Mase had enough and he lifted the gun, steadied his aim and fired at her. She knocked over a lamp on the nightstand and keeled over on the floor. The bullets struck her in the head, the chest and the lower torso. Things were definitely not going as planned.

Then his worst nightmare came true. In the pre-dawn of shallow light coming from the bedroom window, he could see a shadow as the bedroom door swung open. A barrage of shots rang out catching Mase completely by surprise. It dawned on him too late that the old ass security guard had been on to him from the beginning. As Mase stalked he was also being stalked.

BOOM! BOOM! BOOM!

POP! POP!

Shots rang out from close-range as Mase fired back as if on a suicide mission. The old dude dropped after being shot and Mase leaped over him to run out. He was positive the security guard had called backup and he needed to get out before it was too late. Just as he took off running, another shot was fired, hitting him in the ass. The surge of white heat nearly flopped Mase as he stumbled and barely managed to keep his balance.

"I think I got'em! Got him with one of my special Marine bullets! HOO-RAH!" he heard the old security guard exclaim as he lay on the floor.

EIGHT

Fulton County Jail

The cacophony of noise was loud, and so was the stench of unwashed bodies combined with disinfectant and unsolicited fear that was just as much a part of the institution as the wretched of the earth, hardened criminals and poor souls that were forced to live there sometimes for years, innocent until proven guilty.

A mechanical steel door clang shut, echoing as the sound of wooden shoes scraped and chains dragged across the linoleum freshly waxed floors. Lloyd Evans was fitted, shackled with ankle irons and handcuffs, being escorted by two large burly correctional officers. The sporadic sound of their radios resonated as they marched forward with the inmate to the visitation room.

"Man, it better not be no fuckin' cops wanting to talk to me, tell 'em to see my lawyers. A nigga ain't down with dat snitch shit."

"Shut up!" the officer barked.

"Nigga, fuck you!" Lloyd retaliated.

"Keep talking and we'll take your big mouth ass back to your pod with the rest of you crew."

"Man, I don't give a fuck! I'm facing two life sentences and a hundred and seventy-five years! This shit ain't new to me, it's true to me. You know me and my niggaz run this shit," Lloyd aka Black boasted.

The truth of the matter was under jail policy, the guards couldn't deny him a visit and him and his East Point Gangsters did run the jail and were respected by all and feared by most, including some of the guards.

"Yea, when they send your black ass to prison all that is going to change. You gone be somebody's old lady," the guarded chided. The other guard snickered.

Lloyd stopped dead in his tracks, the brawny muscles in his neck from playing Spades for push-ups caused his shoulders to coil and recoiled as he shifted and turned towards the correctional officer and looked at him with an angry scowl.

"Keep it up and I'll have a muthafucka sittin' in yo' yard wit dat chopper one night waiting on your fuck ass. You better check my fuckin' resume. I ain't got shit to lose. Now try a nigga wit' dat fuck shit again."

Silence.

Both correctional officers exchanged wary glances and chuckled, playing it off. They knew Lloyd and his EPG crew were past ruthless. They had filled up a graveyard in the past year alone and were paying off the guards and other staff to smuggle them in drugs.

"Man, it ain't that serious, now move your ass along before I write you up for threatening an officer," the guard said but on a softer tone. He was determined not to back down but he was also now scared for his safety.

"Oh aight, play with it if you want to," Lloyd said in a threatening tone, with grit in his voice and continued to walk.

At the visitation door, the guards radioed that they were outside with an inmate. As soon as they were let inside the transparent lobby, the guards removed his handcuffs but not his leg irons. A door snapped open and an attractive female guard wearing a tight uniform was positioned behind a thick, plastic glass window. She stood with a shocked expression, then waved and spoke through a distorted P.A. system that cracked with static so loud they all flinched and reached for their ears.

"You got a visit in booth nine, Mr. Evans." The correctional officer named LaToya smiled, as she began to smooth her clothes with the palms of her hands. For some reason she couldn't stop smiling.

"Okay thanks, Toya, with yo' sexy ass. Why you don't come through my pod no more?" Lloyd smiled back at her and said in a hushed tone.

LaToya blushed and turned her head. She couldn't have been any older than twenty. She walked off and acted like she didn't hear him, but Lloyd knew he would get at her later. The way she swished her hips as she walked away let him know that she wanted the dick and he was happy to give it to her.

Turning back to the guards walking in front of him, Lloyd moved to the next door and they left.

****

The murmur of voices carried as Lloyd walked awkwardly in the orange jumpsuit and shower slides, fitted in the leg irons. Each small cubicle with people inside, stared; women and children, most of them teary-eyed.

He sat at booth nine as he had been instructed by the female officer and waited. A few of the men with visits threw up the deuces. Lloyd was still that nigga; even behind bars he was running things. But he was a realist. All the wiretaps the Feds and local authorities used against him, he was lucky they wasn't trying to give him a death sentence due to all the conspiracy charges, too, when he was heard ordering hits on rivals.

It bet not be one of them fuck ass police visiting me again talking about a deal to testify, Lloyd thought as he drummed his fingers on the metal counter.

Then a ray of hope hit him as he peered around the booth and saw some ugly nigga with a fine ass bitch. Maybe his baby mama, Dior had finally come to pay him a visit, even though he had shattered a bone in her face. Since she had given birth to the baby she had got ghost on a nigga. Rumor was she ran off with his cousin Kenyon and they was living plush somewhere in Norcross, Georgia. Fuck nigga! From what he had heard, Kenyon had also turned state on him, prepared to testify.

A tall shadow fell over Lloyd and he looked up to see his hatchet face lawyer, Whiffenback, a Jew. The man had the worst case of acne he had ever seen and not just that. He had paid the punk ass lawyer nearly seven hundred thousand. The last time they talked the attorney ask him to consider to take a deal for thirty years. He'd be out in twenty eight with good behavior.

The lawyer had a shit-eating grin as he sat down and placed his some folders on the metal table between them.

"Man, I hope you got some good muhfuckin' news or done brought a nigga a handcuff key, a hacksaw uh s'umtin to get out this bitch," Lloyd said with a frown like he was dead ass serious.

"I do," the lawyer beamed.

"You do what?" Lloyd asked.

"I do have good news for you."

"What you did, bring a nigga a handcuff key and a hacksaw?" Lloyd asked leaning forward as he whispered up at the small mash metal hole in the plastic glass designed to talk.

"No, but there has been a huge break in your case because of the private investigator."

"You talkin' 'bout that muhfucka we hired for three hundred dollars an hour who ain't done shit?!" Lloyd spat.

"Actually, he has. He did some digging and discovered that two homicide detectives by the name of West and Burns had your car and phone bugged with listening devices—"

"Well fuck, it don't take no damn rocket scientist to figure that shit out. I could have told him that. That's how they were able to build the case against me along with the rat ass cousin of mine, Kenyon."

"The problem is from listening to the tapes and examining other incriminating evidence, the Fulton County Police Department's indictment and your arrest was illegal according to the Fourth Amendment. Our records and their records clearly indicate the first evidence submitted was a taped conversation where you ordered Cole Henderson's murder. You were heard ordering his tongue and hands to be cut off and the head dropped on the doorstep of one of your adversaries."

"I told you that wasn't my voice," Lloyd interjected, but he was wearing a smirk on his face that said otherwise as he rubbed on the short hair of his beard while he thought of that day.

"It doesn't matter. From looking at the date the phone conversation was recorded, there wasn't an order granting them to legally record your conversation on March 10. The Fulton County Police didn't get an order until May twenty-first."

The lawyer was on to something. Lloyd slid closer in his seat. "So what you sayin'?"

"I am about to file Habeas Corpus. The police are in violation of the Fourth Amendment to the United States Constitution. That is the part of the Bill of Rights that prohibits unreasonable searches and seizures and requires any warrant to be judicially sanctioned and supported by a judge. So I'm filing a habeas corpus to get you out of here this week."

"Nigga, file that Happy Cockus or whatever the fuck it's called ASAP. I'm ready to get out this bitch and do what I gotta do," Lloyd said. He was too hype.

KEISHA & TRIGGA 2

The lawyer gave him a tacit nod of confidence with his paper thin lips pressed tightly. Both his boubous nose and face were covered with red angry acne bumps, so bad that some of the bumps had white heads that looked like pus inside.

"When you filing that shit?" Lloyd asked, as he anxiously rubbed his hands together.

"The first thing in the morning."

"How long will it take the judge to rule on it?"

"He can rule that day or the next, but since the severity is so crucial, I wouldn't be surprised if he didn't rule on it the same day."

"Then I get to go home."

"Quite possibly, but there is one major problem."

"Problem? Fuck you talkin' 'bout?" Lloyd scuffed and stood up.

"Like in about ninety-nine percent of these cases the prosecution refiled criminal charges."

"Can they do that?"

"In your particular case they can because you have a confidential informant that went to the grand jury against you. Your cousin, Kenyon."

"Fuck Kenyon's bitch ass!" Lloyd exclaim angrily. Then he thought for a minute. "What about if he were to disappear?"

"So would your problem and I have an address here the private investigator stumbled across while he was at the police station." The lawyer reached into his briefcase and removed a sheaf of papers and dug through them.

"Address for what?" Lloyd asked bubbling with excitement. This was too good to be true. If there was a God he shined on Gangstaz and Jack Boys.

"An address to where Kenyon and your wife, Dior are living in Norcross," the lawyer said with a sheepish grin. Lloyd couldn't contain his joy.

"I need dat information ASAP!" Lloyd said and banged his fist down on the metal booth causing the lawyer to flinch nervously.

Wiffenbach gave him the information to where his wife and cousin Keyon were staying. They talked briefly about the upcoming proceedings and the lawyer left.

Lloyd was escorted back to his pod. The entire time he walked down the halls he threw up his set to all the homies he recognized in the connected pods he passed, and talked big shit to the guards. He was on his way home.

****

Once he was back in his pod, he marched right to his cell. He didn't tell any of the homies about his predicament of possibly earning his freedom that week. The fact was he had a real chance of going home, but he didn't trust some of them. A gangstaz first G code is the element of surprise. If the judge let him out, he wasn't telling anybody.

As he moped across the pod, some of his crew asked him was he good, meaning they wanted to know how his visit went. He nodded, gave dap to a few and bounced straight to his cell and closed the door, placing a bed sheet up so nobody could see inside.

He reached deep into his mattress and retrieved his iPhone and made a call he was uncertain of, but with a new hope of life back on the bricks, he had to crank shop back up and find out what the business was on the streets.

NINE

"Nigga, wuz up?" Mase answered the phone just as it was about to go to voicemail.

At the time, he was in a fleabag motel with an obese, dark-skinned chick named Leona. She had two rolls of belly like a beer gut and stretch marks running across her body like a map of the United States. Her chest was flat as a board. She was in her forties but told him she was twenty-two when she chatted with him on the online escort site.

When she showed at his motel room, she actually looked much older than forty, wearing a blond wig and leggings that came damn near up to her chest. There was something peculiar about her that Mase just couldn't put his finger on. Besides, he was horny and had paid to fuck much worse. In addition, one thing that was for certain, she could suck good dick, best he'd ever had for $40. Now he just needed to get her out them leggings to get some ass.

A blunt burned on the nightstand next to a bottle of Cîroc. At the time of the call, she was standing behind him, as he lay with his ass tooted up in the air and his pants around his knees, while she applied some type of cream the doctor had given him for the infection in his ass.

"I'm good, other than the fact a dog that might'a had rabies bit me and I was shot in the ass. Fuckin' gun was so old the ancient bullets may have given me gangrene and the doctor talking about amputating one side of my butt cheeks," he said sarcastically and winced as Leona rubbed his ass softly with massive hands.

But if he were honest, that wasn't his only problem; he was sad and moping over killing his own twin brother.

Disgusted, Lloyd took the phone from his ear and squinted at the number on the screen as if to make sure he dialed the correct number.

This nigga got the worst fuckin' luck on the planet for real, he thought.

"What about the little situation with your brother and that Queen bitch? That's a hundred million dollar lick."

"I murked that nigga already. Man, I ain't gone lie, a nigga a lil' tore up about that shit…" Mase's voice cracked as he spoke and his words trailed off.

"Nigga, get out your damn feelings! Now what happened?"

"Shit, nigga, I'm grieving! Can you blame me?" Mase sniffled and then swallowed hard. If he was looking for sympathy, he was trying to get it from the wrong one. "Anyways, I spoke with Queen. She has a job for us but she was pissed because I told her my brother Trigga missing. I can't tell her he's dead because she won't fuck with me—"

"Are you serious, you really whacked dat fuck nigga and you in talks with Queen?" Lloyd asked, amped up.

"Yeah, man," Mase responded like he was in doldrums as he thought about Trigga.

"Good, now listen. There is a chance I might be getting out this week. Now that nigga dead, we gotta hurry with the plan to take his body to Queen and swap it for mine—"

"We can't do that," Mase revealed to him.

"Why?"

"Because after I murked that nigga, some old ass security guard bust up in the room and shot me in my ass! I had to leave his body there! Ouch! Heavy ass hands, girl. Go slow, take it easy!" Mase admonished to Leona and looked back catching her drinking out the Cîroc bottle and messaging him with one hand.

"WHAT DA FUCK?!" Lloyd yelled out. Then remembering where he was, he looked around and tried to lower his voice and speak calmly. "So you murked the nigga but don't have the fuckin' body? What the hell we supposed to do about the plan?"

"We can use another body," Mase suggested as he winced from the pain in his ass as Leona continued to massage him. He began to get frustrated. "Shit, I don't know what da fuck we can do, man! My ass fuckin' killin' me!"

I can't wait to get rid of this fuckin' idiot, Lloyd thought to himself.

"It's okay. I know who we can use. And he kinda looks like that pretty ass nigga, too. Same height and all," Lloyd said, thinking about his cousin. Kenyon had turned rat and had an appointment coming soon to meet his maker.

"Okay, I'm cool because you still owe me big time for takin' care of all this shit on my own since you been locked up."

Mase flinched again and looked back at Leona. She had lit one of his Black & Mild cigars, the last one in the box and some of the ash fell on his backside.

"Fuck you doin'?" Mase scuffed.

"What it look like I'm doing?" Leona said while using her palm to half-massage his butt cheek with her massive hand.

Mase focused in on her hand for the first time since she started massaging him.

"You smoking my muthafuckin' last cigar n' hurtin' me with them heavy ass hands. Bitch, don't make me slap the fuck out yo' ugly ass."

"Hold up now, nigga. You ain't finna put yo' dick beaters on me!" Leona said with a thick booming baritone voice that resonated so loud it sent shockwaves throughout the dank motel room.

Mase's balls shriveled up into his stomach. He quickly withdrew his ass from Leona's massive hand, as it suddenly occurred to him what was so particular about Leona. *She* was really a *he*!!

"Fuck nigga, you a dude?!" Mase said while holding his ass cheek tenderly as he thought about how he'd just been taken advantage of by Leona. Or maybe he should say Leonard?

"Nigga, don't play dumb. You saw my ad on the internet escort service where it said plain as day, 'transsexual'," Leona said with a voice that was uncannily similar to James Earl Jones. He snaked his massive head so hard the wig nearly toppled off and, from what Mase could see underneath, 'Leonard' was bald as an eagle.

"Whaaaat!? Transsexual? Nigga, I thought that was some type of dance you did…like some extra freaky 'no hands' type shit!"

"I am freaky. Didn't I suck your dick and let you cum in my mouth—"

WHAM!

Before Leona could finish the statement, Mase swung on him with all his might, right upside the head.

"Yo, Mase! What's going on?" Lloyd asked and took the phone away from his ear.

He couldn't believe what he was hearing. When he put the phone to his ear again, all he heard was some scuffling. Mase was involved in the fight of his life. Leona was most definitely a man who had a good set of hands. He could *fight*.

"Man, don't tell me this dumb ass nigga gay too," Lloyd said to himself, not believing what he was hearing.

He disconnected the phone and shook his head, before tossing it back into his hiding spot. He had things to do. He was about to be out in a matter of days and he needed to plan for what he was about to do once he got on the outside. First in his mind was dealing with that nigga, Kenyon. Then he wanted to see his daughter and figure out what the hell he was going to do with Dior.

TEN

"Hello?" Trigga grumbled into the phone after pushing it against his ear.

He felt like shit. He had a crook in his neck and his body was sore. He groaned loudly as he listened in the phone for whoever was on the other end to respond. He checked the caller ID before he answered so he knew it was an Atlanta number, but he didn't know who it was. The only reason he answered because he thought it may have been Tasha, although he prayed it wasn't. Keisha was a handful enough. Juggling Tasha's feelings as well as whatever he had going on with Keisha, was too much even for a nigga like him. He'd dealt with a lot but women were a totally different type of situation that he wasn't used to.

"Is this Mr. Bivens?"

Trigga's eyes shot open at the sound of a man's voice on the other side of the phone. He sat straight up on the lumpy couch that he'd been sleeping on and pressed his ear closer to the phone's speaker.

"Who the fuck is askin' and how you get this number?"

"This is Detective West and I need you to come into the police station immediately. We need to question you concerning two murders that occurred at your room at the W Hotel last night," Detective West finished.

He turned to his partner and winked his eye at Burns, right before he tossed back a handful of Skittles down his thick throat. Burns chewed the candy and then showed off a toothy grin that showcased his blue and red stained teeth. West rolled his eyes and shook his head before turning back to Trigga's voice on the phone.

"I ain't have nothin' to do wit' no fuckin' murders! I wasn't even at my room last night! You must got the wrong—" Trigga's voice trailed off as the realization of what must have happened fell on him.

He wasn't in his room the night before but he knew who was. The homeless couple that he'd given the key card to his room had been. He'd allowed them to stay there because, until Keisha called him begging to be with him, he'd planned on being stationed outside her apartment and sleep in his car all night. It wasn't until she begged to be with him that he decided to check into another luxurious hotel room and take her there to redo their first date.

"Who was murdered?" Trigga asked finally although he already knew the answer.

"A poor ole homeless couple. The husband was murdered in his sleep and the wife was shot to death after waking up. She must have been alarmed when she saw the shooter," West told him.

Trigga closed his eyes and tried to wipe away the image of how happy they had been to get the key to his room, out of his mind. He'd thought he was doing them a good deed but he'd actually led them right to their death. When he opened his eyes, Keisha was standing in front of him wearing one of his large white tees. Her eyes probed his as she stared at him with so much care and concern that he couldn't bear it. He looked away.

"I ain't have nothin' to do wit' that shit," Trigga said again.

"I understand," West told him. "So I'm sure you don't have a problem with coming down to the precinct so we can get that on record."

Trigga pulled the phone away from his face and hit the button to end the call. He wasn't going down to no fuckin' precinct and he was done talking to the cops. He was done with all the shit that had happened in Atlanta so far. Too much bad shit was happening and too many lives had been affected. It was time for him to leave. He'd just have to tell Queen that he couldn't complete the mission. It was time to go. He'd take Keisha with him and he'd deal with Mase later.

"What's wrong?" Keisha asked him.

She walked over and stood in front of him. The scent of vanilla lingered in the air and mixed with another smell that made his dick hard. She was standing right in front of him, and her pussy was inches away from his face. He could smell her natural juices from where he sat and he knew she didn't have any panties on. Without even noticing his actions, he licked his lips and leaned a little closer to take in more of the smell of her womanly essence. He was hornier than a muthafucka.

The night before he had wanted to fuck but it didn't seem right. Keisha wanted him to make a move, and he did too. But even after taking a shower and washing the scent of Tasha off of him, something still wasn't right. He couldn't make himself make love to Keisha after fuckin' Tasha. Something just seemed grimy about that. So instead, he'd lay in the bed with Keisha, spooning her in his arms until he could tell from the light snores escaping her, that she was sleeping peacefully. Then he and his rock hard dick went out to the living room where he lay on the couch and had the most uncomfortable sleep of his lifetime.

"Hello? I asked what's wrong," Keisha repeated.

Trigga opened his mouth to answer, but she distracted him when she shifted suddenly and crossed her arms in front of her chest, as she rocked from heel to heel. There was that delicious, sensual smell again. She had to know what she was doing. Leaning back so he could get his thoughts straight, Trigga looked her in the face and shook his head.

"It's nothing. I have a call that I need to make," he said. "Then I'll go get you some breakfast."

Keisha stared at him for a minute and he saw the wheels in her head turning. She was trying to decide if she was going to pry further for the truth or let him go with his lie. She chose the latter and swiveled around on her heels.

"Fine, I'm going to go take a shower," she said.

She walked away but the scent of her lingered. Trigga couldn't take it anymore. His dick was hard as hell and the sweet scent of her femininity was too much for him to ignore a second longer. Standing up, he walked up behind her and grabbed her by her waist, making her stop in her tracks. He pushed up against her, pressing his hardness against her round ass.

Keisha sucked in a breath and held it, as she felt his manhood press hard into her butt. When he dipped his head into the crook of her neck and kissed lightly on her, a soft moan escaped her lips. She was so sexually frustrated that it wasn't funny. She wanted Trigga so badly but he was being an absolute gentleman for whatever reason, and he didn't even make a move on her the night before. She lay in the bed with him all night, purposefully tooting her ass back towards him to tease him but he didn't bite.

Finally she recognized that he wasn't going to try anything and she went to sleep. When she woke up, expecting him to be in the bed next to her, she peeked out the room and saw him sleeping on the small sofa in the living room. She had half a mind to wake him up and make him come to bed with her. He looked so uncomfortable because the sofa was about a foot shorter than his long, slender body. Seeing him squished on the flat, shapeless cushions almost made her back hurt by just looking.

"You feel me?" Trigga asked her breathlessly.

Swallowing hard, Keisha gave him a small nod and took a deep breath. He brought his hand forward and ran it lightly over the front of the shirt she was wearing, lightly grazing her hardened nipple. She sucked in a breath again and held it in anticipation for what was about to happen. Then Trigga released her waist from his grasp and walked by her into the bathroom, leaving her paralyzed in place by her desire as she watched him turn the corner.

Wait...what? she thought when she heard him turn on the water. Once again, he'd brought her to the precipice of desire and left her hanging. She was pissed.

As Trigga placed his hand under the running water, he cursed himself for the millionth time since he picked Keisha up the day before. This time his reasoning was different from the rest of the times. The other times he was cursing himself because he wanted to have sex with her but knew he shouldn't. This time he cursed himself because he wanted to have sex with her but he couldn't. He was a second away from tearing the shirt off of her body and pushing up into her when he realized that he was out of condoms. He'd used his last one on Tasha.

Fuck! he yelled to himself in his mind.

This shit was getting frustrating. Never in his life did he want a woman so bad. Part of him was saying 'fuck the condom' and just raw-dog her. He knew Keisha and the type of person she was. She seemed clean. But if he were honest with himself, he knew a STD wasn't what he was afraid of. He knew once he got in her, there would be no stopping. And with the bullshit ass luck he'd been having, she'd be pregnant off one time.

Reaching on the counter, he grabbed the bubble bath that was left courtesy of the hotel, and dumped nearly half the bottle in the tub. As he watched it fill up with bubbles, he tried to extinguish the thoughts in his mind of how Keisha would look sitting in the tub butt-naked in only a few more minutes. Closing his eyes, he shook his head and tried not to think on it.

"Can I get in now?" a small voice said from behind him. Trigga was still standing with his hands in his pants pocket, staring at the nearly full tub with the image of Keisha's naked body partially covered with bubbles in his mind, when he heard her speak behind him. Turning halfway, he looked over his shoulder to tell her that she could and almost fell over when he saw that she was standing right behind him wearing not a stitch of clothing.

Man, fuck that condom.

Trigga walked slowly over to her and, without saying a word, scooped her right up into his arms. She wrapped her legs around him and pressed her lips against his. Holding tightly to the bottom of her apple-shaped ass, he pulled her tightly into him as he kissed her deeply. She was so wet that he could feel it through the thin material of his shirt. He had to taste her. He couldn't hold back any longer.

As soon as he laid Keisha on the bed, he bent down and parted her sexy, thick thighs. His eyes trained in on the prettiest pussy that he'd ever seen in his life. Her pink lips were wide open exposing the swollen nub in between. Bending down slowly, Trigga went right in for the prize and sucked in into his mouth then ran his tongue back and forth across it as he sucked. Keisha went wild and he had to hold her thighs apart to keep her from closing her legs. The feeling was so good to her, she didn't know whether to make him stop or to beg him to keep going. He had her just that confused.

The orgasm came so fast and was so powerful that she couldn't even catch her breath or will it to go away. She was embarrassed that Trigga brought her to this place so fast, but there was nothing on Earth that would convince her to make him stop.

"Oh Gaaaawwwwwd…." Keisha moaned out loud as she began rolling her hips into his face.

Trigga placed his palms underneath her and pulled her closer to him. When he felt the vibrations in her thighs began to slow down, he stopped suckling on her nub and then stuck his tongue out and pushed it into her. He used his tongue like a spoon and scooped up her sweet nectar from inside until it was all gone.

When Keisha realized what he was doing, it nearly sent her into another wave of an orgasm. Never had a man ever seemed to crave her in the way that Trigga did. To actually make her cum and then suck it down like it was the sweetest thing he'd ever tasted….it drove her crazy. She almost felt like she was in love.

"I want to please you," she whispered as she looked into Trigga's eyes once he pulled up from beneath her. He was so sexy and just the sight of him made her horny all over again. She could go at it with him all day and night if he wanted and she'd never get tired.

"Then lie back and open wide," he said as he dropped his pants down to his ankles.

Keisha's eyes nearly bugged out her head when she saw what he was working with, but she tried to hide her surprise. Trigga had noted it anyways. Doing what she was told, Keisha lay all the way back on the bed and opened her mouth as big as she could get it. She felt Trigga stop moving and then she heard a faint snicker escape his lips so she peeked her eyes open.

"What?" she asked him with a confused expression on her face.

"I meant to open your legs wide, Keesh," he said with another, heavier laugh.

"Oh," Keisha said with a sheepish smile. She laid back down flat on her back and opened her legs as wide as they could go, making a perfect split.

"SHIT!" Trigga cursed as he watched her. "That shit is sexy as fuck."

Keisha smiled and then dropped her legs so that her feet were flat on the bed, but she still gave him full access to her womanhood. She watched with a hint of a smile as he tried to come to terms with what she'd just seen. Now the joke was on him. It had been many years since she'd been a cheerleader but she still had it.

Leaning down over her, Trigga gently pushed the tip of his dick in her and a soft moan escaped her lips once more. The head of his dick was so large that just the motion of him pushing it in sent shivers up her spine. When he continued and pushed the length of himself in her, she had to bite her lip to stop herself from crying out.

"You good?" he asked her softly against her ear, as he began stroking softly into her. She nodded her head quickly as she felt the euphoric feeling that came from great sex washing over her.

She bit down harder on her lip and started twerking her hips against him, against the wishes of her mind. Her mind was telling her to just lie there and not move. She was so close to an orgasm already, she was scared that if she helped him any, she'd be cumming again before he'd even had the chance to really get started.

Trigga's rhythm increased and a cry of pleasure escaped Keisha's lips. Then he bent down and covered her nipple with his mouth as he kept up his rhythm. With his other hand, he pinched her other nipple and it sent shivers through her. She could no longer hold back but neither could he. Like ravaged animals, both of them began humping into each other as they kissed each other forcefully. Keisha bit down on his bottom lip and he pulled hard on her nipple; they enveloped themselves in a mixture of pain and pleasure as they explored each other with a hunger that only the other could satiate.

"Oh my GOD!" Keisha yelled out when she felt herself about to orgasm.

She pushed her head back deep into the pillow behind her and squeezed her eyes tightly shut, as she worked her hips harder and harder onto Trigga's manhood. She felt his strokes get heavier and more forceful. She could tell he was about to cum too.

"Keesh! Fuck…oh God, Keesh," he said just as he was about to cum. Keisha's love was so intense and it felt so good. It was almost like an outer body experience and he didn't want it to end, but his climax was coming and he could do nothing to stop it. Not like he wanted to.

Then, just as the onslaught of the perfect ending to the perfect moment approached him, Trigga opened his mouth and said something that he'd never, ever imagined he would say.

"Keessshhhhhh-uhhh, shit! I fuckin' love you!"

His words were all she needed to hear in order for her to let go. Keisha and Trigga held onto each other so tightly it was almost as if they were one person, as they experienced the most Earth-shattering orgasm they'd ever experienced in their lifetime.

Rolling over to his side, Trigga held onto Keisha from behind and wrapped his arm around her, as he listened to her breathing slow in tempo. In his mind were the words that he'd spoken as he tried to decide whether they were words he meant or words that he'd said only because he had been in the middle of experiencing the greatest feeling on Earth.

Maybe she didn't hear it, he surmised and shook the thought from his mind. The fatigue of their intense lovemaking was settling on him and he felt his eyelids growing heavy.

Just as he was nearly at the point of sleep, Keisha said something that snatched him right out of the beginning stages of slumber and brought him right back into reality.

"Trigga…I love you too."

ELEVEN

"The defendant, Lloyd Evans is free to leave."

Triumphantly, Lloyd's normally emotionless attorney looked over at the prosecutor's table, where his nemeses stood with his eyes wide open in shock and surprise, and pumped his fist.

"Yes! Yes!" Whiffenback yelled out loud before turning to Lloyd who was standing still in place, as if he couldn't believe his freedom had come so easily.

"Next case," the judge said nonchalantly and looked over at the bailiff.

In disbelief, Lloyd sat there stunned. He could barely feel his lawyer pump his hand vigorously as he shook it. Whiffenback was ecstatic that Lloyd was being released and he didn't have to worry about being at the tail end of a street goon's wrath for failing in his mission. Lloyd was happy as well but he knew the worst was yet to come. The Feds still were able to indict him although the State had let him go. He had barely got away by the skin of his teeth. He looked over his shoulder at the two homicide detectives. The fat one, James, was giving him the evil eye as he stood to his feet to leave.

Lloyd knew he had to find Kenyon and find him fast, before the Feds were able to mount a strong case against him using his rat cousin as their key witness. Time was not on his side. And not just that, the stage was set for Queen. If he moved fast enough, he could team up with dumb ass Mase long enough to rob Queen's main stash house, then kill her without anyone even knowing. Since Lloyd was supposedly dead from what Mase had told Queen, no one would even suspect that he had anything to do with it. And after he'd taken all of the money, he'd make sure the only person who knew the truth, that idiot Mase, was dead right along with Queen. But first he had to get to Kenyon.

There was one place he was certain he would find Kenyon. That was the address that his lawyer had given him to where he and Dior were staying along with Lloyd's daughter. It was time to pay them a visit with his crew, before they got word that Lloyd was free and decided to make a move.

Lloyd was escorted back to the pod, to pack his meager belongings in his cell which was normal procedure. Still, his mind was swirling with all of the things he had to do and whether or not he was really free. He was uncertain of his fate. He had heard countless times about stories where guys would be released from jail or prison and the federal marshals would be right there as soon as they walked through the exit of the jail, to scoop them up like an eagle devouring its prey.

The homies and even a few correctional officers showed Lloyd mad love as he packed his gear to leave. Every week, he had

KEISHA & TRIGGA 2

had been spending over five grand paying off guards to do favors for him and to buy honey buns, Snicker bars and more from the canteen for all his EPG crew, who made sure no one gave him any problems. Not to mention the good loud and lean he was able to have smuggled in the jail on the regular for the past few weeks he was there.

His EPG crew on the inside would miss him dearly.

In his cell, he checked his phone to handle some business before giving it to his lil homie, Trav. He was an EPG who was waiting to be transferred to Georgia State Penitentiary to serve a forty-five year bid plus life for a double homicide in a house invasion that went bad. Trav, high off purp and mollies, showed up at the wrong address and killed an innocent father and son thinking they were rival drug dealers. He left a shell casing at the crime scene with his prints on it and was apprehended later.

Lloyd made one last call to one of his most trusted niggas in his EPG crew. The one who he infamously named AK. AK was part of the organized crew within the clique that was called 'Ground Patrol.' Ground Patrol was a code word for what this crew did on the regular: home invasion with a body count.

****

A Few Hours Later

That same day Lloyd Evans took one of the longest treks of his life; it was only a few yards but it felt like eternity. His heart pounded in his chest like thunder ricocheting throughout his body with each step as he left the county jail. The ardent bright sunlight hurt his eyes as he squinted, checking the block for an ambush as he walked over to the waiting candy-red Maserati. With each step he had the uncanny feeling he was being watched by the Feds and they would rush out, guns aimed, and take him into custody by using the RICO Act.

Lloyd made it to the luxury whip with a deep sigh. Still, it was hard for him to believe he had gotten out of jail and was really free. He had a weight on him and, although he tried to shake it, he couldn't. He felt like something was still off kilter. Maybe when he was finally able to put a bullet in Kenyon's skull, this feeling would go away.

His homie, AK, opened the door and joked as he gave him a chest bump and some dap.

"Nigga, what kinda of bird don't fly?" His diamond and gold grill in his mouth sparkled as he spoke.

"Well, sho' ain't a jail bird because nigga I stay fly," Lloyd quipped back and cracked a smile, as he looked around one last time before he dipped inside the whip.

As soon as he got in, sitting on the buttery soft beige Louis Vuitton leather seats was LaToya, the correctional officer from the jail. He had to do a double take when he saw her. She was wearing a Pink Prada silk low-cut blouse that left little to the imagination. She was braless with her erect, strawberry shaped nipples on display. She had on some white coochie cutter shorts cut so scandalous that he could see one of her pussy lips bulging out the middle. She donned six-inch stiletto heels that perfectly complemented her long, curvy brown legs.

LaToya smiled nervously as she mischievously reached for his zipper, hoping he was excited to see her. AK hit a button to bring up the partition and give them some privacy. But, although she looked sexy as hell, pussy was the last thing on Lloyd's mind. He batted away her hands and knocked on the partition to make AK lower it, as LaToya pouted to herself beside him.

I'm back on the bricks, his mind ruminated as the whip pulled away from the jail.

"You good, my nigga?" AK asked looking back over his shoulder from the driver's seat. The potent scent of 'loud' was heavy in the air. Meek Mill and Nicki Minaj's song, "All Eyes on You", played on the radio.

"Naw, I ain't good. I gotta get to this fuck nigga, Kenyon," Lloyd said with his mind deep into his thoughts. He felt LaToya's hands on his pants leg again. He ignored her completely and he could tell it annoyed her.

"Yea, I heard about that foul shit him and old girl, Dior did. We had Ground Patrol put an APB out on the streets for both their asses, but it just seems like the nigga and her pulled a disappearing act."

"Disappearing act? Naw, I already told you exactly what that nigga been up to," Lloyd said, as he batted LaToya's hands away from his zipper.

"Lemme suck it," she coed with lubricious lips so shiny they looked like they had been waxed with chicken grease.

Lloyd shook his head and shot her a threatening stare. She fell back in her seat and went to pouting as AK continued down the road. Neither of them saw the all-black Chrysler Charger three cars behind which contained both homicide cops, West, and his partner, Burns.

AK talked on and gave Lloyd updates on what had been happening on the block since he'd been gone, but he couldn't help admiring LaToya's thick legs and phat ass pussy print, and kept glancing at her through the rearview mirror.

Finally, he wiggled his eyebrows at Lloyd and said, "Shawty thick as fuck!"

LaToya looked up and blushed as she looked out the window, pretending that the compliment didn't mean much to her. Lloyd nodded his head in agreement but something about AK giving her the attention she desired bugged him, so he reached over and put his arm around her neck and pulled her closer to him. When she turned to look at him, he leaned over and gave her a deep kiss making sure to fully explore her hot, sweet mouth with his thick tongue. When he pulled away, he could see the deep affection she had for him in her eyes. Lloyd could see the loyalty that she had for him and he knew she was down for him for real.

"Listen, AK, I'mma drop her off at the crib my nigga, then we going to pick up the homies for some Ground Patrol actions. I have an address in Norcross, Georgia. I hope, just hope it's legit. Time to pay wifey and my fuck ass cousin, Keyon a visit."

AK nodded his head and punched the gas.

TWELVE

Trigga stirred in his sleep when he heard humming. He thought maybe it was coming from a dream until he reached out for Keisha and his hand fell on empty space. She wasn't there. Rolling onto his back, he reached out and stretched while yawning loudly as he heard the joyous sound of a happy and content woman. With a smile on his face, he sat and listened as Keisha hummed a tune, while she splashed around in the bath water that he'd run for her. The song sounded familiar to him but at the moment he couldn't place it. But he knew it was a love song.

Trigga…I love you too.

Her words echoed in his mind as he lay on the bed with his hands behind his head, as he replayed their moments of intense pain, pleasure and love. Trigga couldn't say that he'd ever been in love before. He'd never really been close enough to a woman to call it love. Sure, he'd dated a few bad ass females throughout his time in college, but after he had to drop out and focus on his hustle, he put pussy behind him and focused on making money. Plus, he saw firsthand how irresponsible a female with a fat ass and friendly vagina made Mase, and he didn't want to be like that. So, he never got close enough to a woman for it to happen to him.

And then here comes Keisha. No matter how he tried to distance himself from her, fate made it so that he couldn't let her be. Whether she was following behind him and jumping in his car while he was on a mission to kill, or whether he felt the need to be stationed outside of her apartment to protect her, the fact of the matter was that she was meant to be part of his life. That part was obvious.

Trigga was pulled out of his thoughts by the shrill sound of his phone ringing and he frowned. No one had that number but a few people and he didn't wish to speak with any of them at the moment. When he looked at the caller ID, it was another local Atlanta number. Trigga pressed the button to answer the call, his bad attitude already on the rise because he had a feeling it was the slick-ass detective calling him again.

"What the fuck you want?" Trigga said into the speaker.

He noticed that Keisha stopped humming in the bathroom and he was positive that she'd heard him. Rolling over, he stood up and walked out the balcony adjacent to the bedroom. He didn't want her to be alarmed by anything that she may hear.

"Um…I-I just wanted to talk. I mean…I'm sorry for calling," a small voice said on the other line.

Trigga's mood changed instantly from pissed off to guilty, when he realized that it wasn't the detective on the other line. It was Tasha.

"Shit, Tasha...I didn't know it was you. My bad," Trigga started. He turned around and looked back inside the room. He knew that Keisha wasn't done with her shower but he still felt paranoid as hell for speaking to Tasha while she was just in the other room.

"It's okay. Listen, I was wondering if I could see you some time today. I just...I can't explain how I'm feeling," she said to him and Trigga grinded his teeth together.

You're feelin' clingy. Just like a virgin normally does after a nigga dicks her down right. Fuck! Trigga thought to himself.

"Listen, Tash, I got a lot of stuff goin' on. I can't come over. I'm sorry," he said to her. There was silence on the other line and he felt like shit. "I'm not the one for you. I can promise you that. I'm bad news and I got a lot of shit with me. Go find you some college nigga, fall in love, graduate and get married. Have kids with that nigga and be happy. That's the kinda shit that you want and that's the kinda shit I can't give you."

Even as Trigga said the words, he knew they wouldn't mean shit to Tasha. She was an innocent girl and innocent chicks loved bad boys. And women in general always loved what they felt they couldn't have. People said that men were hunters, but Trigga felt like women were the ultimate hunters. If you tell a woman that she can't get a man or that he is off limits, she would make it her only goal to make a nigga fall in love. Women saw that shit as an accomplishment. Then they would leave that sad ass nigga as soon as they got the chance and run off with the nigga they should have been with all along. That's just how shit worked.

"I gotta go," Trigga said suddenly. The silence on the other end was irritating him because he knew what was happening. Tasha had given him something that she cherished and he'd taken it unknowingly. Now she thought she was in love.

How the fuck did I get myself in this shit? Trigga asked himself. *A month ago ain't nobody love me and now I got two chicks thinkin' that shit. Da fuck?*

Trigga hung up the phone before Tasha got a chance to respond and dialed Queen's number. He had to get the fuck out of Atlanta ASAP. And he was taking Keisha with him whether she knew it or not. That school shit would just have to be transferred to New York. There were plenty of colleges there and he wasn't leaving without her. If he left and she stayed here, it would drive him crazy. There was no other way.

"Trigga?" Queen asked as soon as she picked up the phone.

Her tone was off and Trigga couldn't read it, but he knew she had to be mad as hell that he'd missed the call with Mase yesterday. He wanted to think up an excuse because he couldn't tell Queen he missed talking to her about business because he was diving in some virgin pussy. But then again, Queen would know if he was lying so there was no need to try that either.

"Queen, I'm sorry for missing the call yesterday. I told Mase that we'd call you together but I was…preoccupied with some shit. Anyways, it's too much shit going on down here. I haven't been able to complete the job yet and I gotta pull out. You gotta find somebody else to do it," Trigga told her.

He felt like shit for telling Queen that he'd failed at the one mission that was most important to her. To Queen, there was nothing more important to her than family. The fact that Lloyd had murdered her brother was unforgiveable to her, and she wouldn't stop until he was confirmed to be dead. Trigga had never failed her before and he knew had he been anyone else, she would have issued for him to be killed too. But he hoped that the friendship he'd forged with her would allow her to have some mercy.

"What I'm trying to figure out is what the fuck you are talkin' about," Queen started. Trigga's eyebrows rose up in the air. This was not the response that he'd been expecting.

"The call—"

"Yes, I know you missed the call. I spoke with Mase last night and he told me that Lloyd was dead and you were missing in action which was why you weren't on the call. He said that he shot him in the head in some hotel and would deliver the body to me by next week. So my question to you is what the hell are you sayin, Lloyd is not dead?"

Before Trigga could respond, the line went dead. Turning towards the room, he saw Keisha standing in the room naked as she dried off. She smiled at him and blew him a kiss but he didn't return the gesture. She frowned when she saw the stern look on his face as he stared at her, but Trigga still didn't respond. His mind was swirling with thoughts regarding the conversation that he'd just had with Queen.

Mase called her last night? He said that he'd killed Lloyd inside of a hotel room? But Lloyd is in jail.

Then the words that Lloyd had spoken to him on that dark, dreary night came back to his memory. They were the words that Lloyd said as he held the gun to Trigga's skull right after Keisha's shrill scream had pierced the midnight sky.

"How about this…I collect the mill on my head from that Queen bitch and use your body as mine."

Those were Lloyd's words. That's what he'd said. And now according to Queen, Mase had promised to deliver his body to her the same night that the homeless couple had been killed in his hotel room. There was the confirmation that he'd needed to put his thoughts to rest. Mase *was* working with Lloyd and together, they were planning to kill him and take the money.

Trigga clenched his jaw together and, in a matter of seconds, all of the emotion, loyalty, brotherly love and regard that he had for Mase was erased. Mase was no longer family to him, he was his enemy and also, along with Lloyd, he was his next mission. But first he had to get Keisha to safety and that meant they had to move out of the hotel that he'd booked in his name. If it had been so easy for the police to find his last one, he was sure that Lloyd would be able to pull some strings in his city to find out about the one they were in now.

The only thing that he wondered was did Mase tell Queen that he had disappeared because he had actually thought he'd killed him or was that just what he'd told her so that she wouldn't question why Trigga wasn't on the call? He couldn't be sure so he had to get Keisha out. But first he needed to text Queen.

I'll get to the bottom of this and get it settled. I'm back on it.

He knew she wouldn't respond so he didn't wait for her to. He just pushed the phone into his pocket and walked into the room.

"What's wrong?" Keisha asked him once he walked inside.

"Nothing. We gotta go," he told her. He walked over and grabbed his duffle bag from off the floor and started stuffing all of their belongings in it, mixing his with Keisha's.

"Right now?" she asked as she spread lotion on her legs. "Why?"

"Because I said so. Get dressed. Put on the shit you had on yesterday. I'll buy you some new clothes when we get to New York," he muttered as he tossed her pink lace panties at her.

"NEW YORK?!" Keisha half-yelled.

She stood up and looked at him like he was crazy and placed her hand on her hip. Then, thinking twice about the tattoo of Lloyd's name on her ass that she'd hidden from Trigga so far, she sat down and snatched the panties off the bed and pulled them on.

"I can't go to New York with you, Trigga," she said sadly as she pulled on her clothes. "I know you have to leave. I know you don't live here...and I'm fine with that, or at least I have to be. You can just drop me off at home and I'll see you when I see you."

Keisha was saying all the right things but she didn't believe it. What she'd said about Trigga after they'd made love was the truth...she did feel that she loved him. And for that brief moment in time, she forgot that he was only in Atlanta for work and that he had to one day leave. She didn't think that she would be hearing from him a few minutes later that he would have to go. But she couldn't complain about something that she knew was going to happen.

"Keesh, I think you are misunderstanding me," Trigga responded as he zipped up the duffle bad.

Keisha noticed that he didn't move to take any of her stuff out of the bag before he zipped it and was hot and ready to dish out an attitude.

"Trig—"

"I ain't fuckin'askin' you to go with me to New York right now. I'm tellin' you that's what the fuck you doin'!" he told her matter-of-factly then he tossed the bag over his shoulder and beckoned with his hand for her to hurry up.

"What? Listen, I don't know you like that!"

Trigga sighed out loud. She was trying his patience and this wasn't the time. But whether he had to bend her over his shoulder and carry her out or not, one thing was for certain was that Keisha was definitely walking her ass out of the hotel room with him, getting in the car, then hopping on a plane and flying to New York with him.

"Lloyd is out of prison," he told her. It was a lie but he said it anyways.

As far as he knew, Lloyd was still locked up with the possibility of getting out, but he wasn't out yet. However, he had to say whatever he could to get Keisha to stop bucking and do what he needed her to do. And it looked like it had worked.

Keisha's mouth dropped open and she thought long and hard about what Trigga had just said.

Lloyd was out? How the hell did he manage that?

"He's out and I have to leave for New York now. I need you to stay there until I handle this shit with him and Mase. Then you can come back and live as you please. But I need to make sure you're safe," Trigga told her.

It was a lie. Once she was in New York, he didn't plan on her ever coming back. He planned on setting things up for her so nicely there that Atlanta would only be a faint memory. But she didn't have to know that yet.

"Okay," Keisha agreed with tears in her eyes. She felt the feeling of panic come back to her. It was a feeling that she had been able to push away since being in Trigga's presence. He calmed her and made her feel safe. But it was times like these when she was reminded that she was actually in danger.

"What about Tish?" she asked him after she was fully dressed and ready to go. "My apartment is in my name. I don't want her to get hurt."

"I'll make sure she's good. Don't worry," Trigga assured her. She wrinkled her brow and gave him a look like she doubted him. "I promise."

His vow was enough for her. Grabbing her purse off the table, Keisha reached for Trigga's hand as they walked to the door. It was something that felt so natural to her, holding his hand but she felt him jump and toss a quick glance in her direction so she knew it caught him by surprise. However, instead of pulling away, he squeezed her tiny hand and held on firmly as they stepped into the elevator.

The hotel lobby was incredibly busy as they walked out the elevator and something about the crowd made Keisha feel nervous. She was anxious to get to the car and away from the crowd. There was no telling who all was around them and who all was watching. Lloyd had eyes all over the city. If he was after them, it would be hard to avoid him or his goons.

When they stepped out the doors of the hotel, the bright rays of the sun made her squint. It was a beautiful day but something felt off about it. She couldn't even fully enjoy it or the man's whose hand she was clutching who stood right beside her. All she could think was that Trigga was right; they had to get the hell out of Atlanta. She didn't know what he meant when he said that he had to 'handle' the situation with Lloyd and his brother, but she knew that the way he said it made her shiver and she wasn't sure she even wanted to know.

"Well, look what we have here!" a voice exclaimed from behind them.

Keisha felt her heart skip a beat in her chest as her eyes widened in shock, alarm and fear, as she clutched tightly onto Trigga's hand. They'd been found. Her fear was being realized. One of Lloyd's goons had stumbled upon them and they would be gunned down right in the middle of the street.

THIRTEEN

Trigga grinded his teeth together as he looked into the eyes of Detective West as he and his partner, Detective Burns approached him and Keisha right in front of the doors of the hotel. Once again these nosey ass pretend-cops were causing trouble for him. Why the hell were they in his face instead of trying to track down the muthafucka they'd let get away was beyond him.

"So....you're Maurice Bivens AKA Trigga and you're..." West's voice trailed off as he did a horrible job pretending like he was thinking. "Oh, I know! You're Keisha O'Neal! Ms. O'Neal, you certainly look like you've recovered well!"

Keisha squinted at the white men in front of her as she tried to figure out where she knew them. Then it dawned on her suddenly. They were the cops who had questioned her at the hospital.

"Are you all goin' somewhere?" Burns asked as he walked up and looked pointedly at the duffle bag over Trigga's shoulder. "You're packing a little heavy, to be headed to the precinct to answer our question about the double homicide in your other hotel room last night."

Keisha turned sharply to look at Trigga with surprise in her eyes and a confused expression on her face. Trigga clenched and unclenched his jaw as he stared straight ahead without saying a word or returning her stare. He felt her pull her hand away from his and tried to ignore the slight pang in his heart. Though it was a small act, to him it felt like the first act of betrayal.

Double homicide? Keisha thought to herself as her heart pounded in her chest. *In his hotel room?*

"Oh, so I'm guessing Mr. Bivens didn't fill you in on the news, huh Ms. O'Neal?" West opened his mouth and let out a dry cackle.

"And what do we have here?" Burns said as he moved close to Trigga. Trigga snatched away and yelled out but it was too late.

"Muhfucka, get da fuck away from—" He stopped when he saw Burns waving his pistol in his hand. He'd pulled it from his hiding spot at the base of Trigga's back.

"I can almost guarantee that this isn't registered to you. Either way," he said as he handed it off to his partner, careful to only handle it between his thumb and forefinger. "We're going to have to take it in and run some tests on it."

"Hey, Burns….it's a Glock nine. Same gun that killed the homeless couple in your hotel last night!" West smiled deeply as if he'd just cracked the code to the world's hardest puzzle.

"Well, is that so?" Burns said sarcastically.

In a matter of seconds, he'd pulled out his handcuffs and his partner West had moved in on Trigga. Trigga muttered some words, but he knew better than to resist. Burns and his shady partner, West, had been wanting to find a reason to lock him up for months. There wasn't an inch of doubt in his mind that if he resisted, they would only be happy to pad on extra charges once they found out that the gun he had on him was actually registered and was clean. It couldn't be linked to any bodies. Not any that had been found anyways.

"Maurice Bivens, you are under arrest for the murder of Geraldine and Paul Pickney…"

As they placed the cuffs on Trigga's wrists, making sure to be especially rough with him while they did it, Trigga looked over at Keisha. She was standing totally still but the expression on her face was one of hurt and confusion but also fear. She had no idea what was going on. One minute everything was perfect and then in the next second, it was like everything was at the other end of the spectrum.

"Go home," Trigga said to her as they pulled him towards their unmarked vehicle. "I'll be out and I'll call you soon. Remember what I gave you!"

Keisha watched with her lips partially open as they roughly pushed Trigga into the backseat of the black police car and drove off at high speeds with their sirens blaring and the lights flashing. People who had been standing around watching the entire incident began to whisper and stare as they walked away.

"Excuse me, ma'am," someone said from around her. "He dropped these."

It wasn't until the car had disappeared out of her sight that Keisha turned her attention to the voice of the person speaking to her. She looked into the sad eyes of an older white man, who looked about forty years old. His hand was outstretched and he was holding something in it out to her. Keisha looked inside and then opened her own palm for him to drop the contents into her hand.

It was the car keys to Trigga's ride.

"Thank you," she said quietly. The white man gave her a tight-lipped smile and then walked away.

Tearful and afraid, Keisha turned around, holding the keys tightly in her hand and walked towards the parking garage to the car. She had no idea what she would do other than obey Trigga's last words. She was going to go home, lock herself inside and make sure that she'd kept the gun he'd given her close by.

FOURTEEN

"What the fuck you mean 'we gotta move *right now*', Kenyon? Why so urgent all of a sudden?" Dior asked as she stared into Kenyon's face with her brows furrowed. She was holding Karisma in her arms and the baby was cooing loudly as she looked at Kenyon, almost as if she were trying to figure out what was wrong with him herself.

Kenyon was standing in front of Dior with a fear-stricken look on his face, and she didn't know why, but it bothered her seeing the man who had been so strong and powerful in stature and character, turn into the person who was in front of her now. He looked bothered and stressed out but she didn't understand why. Everything with Lloyd was over, from what she knew. He was in prison and facing three life sentences. Everything was going according to plan.

"We have to go," he said again.

He closed his eyes and ran his hands over his face. He was stressed to the max and he didn't want to tell Dior why. Up to this point, she'd had faith in him as a man and the decisions that he made. He didn't want that to change but the reality of the situation is that he had greatly underestimated Lloyd's reach. Earlier that day, he'd walked out of the police station and he saw one of the East Point gang members standing outside.

Normally, he wouldn't think anything of seeing some of his street partners around town. But the fact that he was walking out of the police station, and the way the man twisted up his fingers to form a gun as he aimed it at Kenyon, put him on notice. Somehow his greatest fears had been realized; Lloyd knew that he had turned snitch and he'd told the crew. If they found out where he lived with his family, they would all be dead.

Scared beyond belief for his life as well as Dior's and Karisma's, Kenyon had ran over to the nearest stash house, gunned down the few men that were in there and stole all the money inside. He needed a large amount of cash on hand so he could get Dior and Karisma out of the state as soon as possible. The only reason he'd stayed was so that he could testify against Lloyd and make sure that he'd be locked up forever. But right now, he wasn't concerned with all of that. Lloyd was in jail and still was able to make moves as if he were on the streets. Kenyon had to leave.

"Listen, Dee. I got something I gotta tell you," he started. He sighed heavily as Dior looked at him with curious but caring eyes. He had no resolution in mind now but to tell her the truth. It was the only way that he could get her to understand the importance of them leaving.

"What is it?" she started. Karisma reached up and grabbed at her mother's breast, indicating that she was hungry. Dior pulled her blouse down and Kenyon waited until Karisma was suckling happily before he continued.

"I...I started workin' with the state to get Lloyd locked up. They asked me to testify to make sure that he stays in prison." Dior's eyes opened wide and her brows shot straight up in the air.

"YOU are testifying against LLOYD?!" Dior yelled out. Karisma frowned up her cute little face at her mother's loud voice but kept right on suckling.

"I had to! He was going to get out on a technicality if I didn't! I had to make sure that he didn't and he couldn't come after us!" Kenyon tried to reason with her. Dior shook her head angrily.

"You didn't have to do shit, Ken...that wasn't the plan. The plan was for us to skip town and leave...go somewhere where he couldn't find us! Is that why we're still here?"

When Kenyon didn't answer, she knew the truth. The reason they were still in Atlanta instead of across seas somewhere was because Kenyon had turned into a rat.

"I can't fuckin' believe this! Snitches get stitches...do you think that shit is fake? You know how many muthafucka's I've seen get gutted up for that shit...right in my fuckin' living room! You're Lloyd's cousin. You know he has eyes everywhere!"

Kenyon nodded sadly as she spoke. Everything that she was saying was true. He had greatly underestimated Lloyd's reach and authority but when Karisma was born, he became desperate and did something that he normally wouldn't have done. He was only trying to protect his family.

"I was only tryin' to protect you two. With Lloyd out, we'd always be living in fear that he'd find a way to come after us. You think that nigga really gone stop lookin' for us just because we globetrotted to another location? You got his fuckin' child, Dior! If he can't get to us, he'll send a message by gunnin' down your mom and pops. This is the streets and Lloyd is a goon…he don't play by the rules. I was just doin' what the fuck I felt I had to do!"

Tears filled Dior's eyes as she listened to Kenyon speak. He was right and she knew he was right because in the time that she'd been with Lloyd, she'd seen him do things to people's families that made her shudder. Innocent people had paid the price of their loved ones decisions plenty of times and she'd heard Lloyd order the kills. He had no mercy and didn't give two fucks about anyone.

"This is too much," Dior whispered as tears fell down her cheeks. Kenyon cupped her face in his hands and kissed her lightly on the lips.

"Baby, I know and I'm sorry. I fucked up. But we gotta go…I have to get you and Karisma out of here. I could never forgive myself if something happened to the two of you," he said. "I'll come back and handle this shit after y'all are safe."

Dior nodded slowly and looked down at her daughter. She was sleeping quietly with her mouth still wrapped loosely around Dior's nipple.

"Why don't you relax for a minute…I'm going to take a drive. I need to clear my mind and get things in order for us to get out of here. I promise, I'll make sure that everything is alright. Do you trust me?" he asked her.

Dior looked up into his eyes and smiled weakly. She did love him and she did trust him. But at that moment, she couldn't help the nagging feeling that she had placed her trust in the wrong cousin. The one who couldn't protect her.

***

There was something about a bubble bath that always calmed Dior. During the time that she'd been a mother, she hadn't had the chance to enjoy that luxury. Karisma was a beautiful baby and she wouldn't trade her for the world, but she was a hand full. She was just like her father; she wanted everything immediately and she wanted it her way. Kenyon always bent to her will and was only too eager to make his little princess happy but, although Dior did the same, it was exhausting.

She'd contemplated getting a nanny a few times to help her, but Kenyon always made her feel guilty when she suggested it, saying that she was a strong woman and he knew she could do it on her own. He said that he didn't want Karisma bonding with any woman other than her and that she shouldn't want it either. So she pushed the thought away and moved forward with taking care of her very demanding daughter without complaint.

Dior's ear piqued when she heard a noise and she sat still to listen hard for any additional movement. Kenyon had only been gone about fifteen minutes and she knew that he couldn't have returned that quickly unless he'd forgotten something. When she didn't hear anything else, she laid her head back down on the edge of the tub and continued enjoying her soak. But then the sound of Karisma's laughter interrupted her peace, and she groaned a little to herself. She loved to hear her daughter laugh, but now she knew her few moments alone in peace were over. She had to get up and tend to the princess.

Dior stood up, stepped out of the tub and wrapped her towel tightly around her body after drying off. She looked around for her robe and grabbed it from the hook behind her bathroom door and carried it with her into the bedroom, where she lotioned up quickly and then placed the robe over her shoulders. After securing it by tying it into a bow in front of her, she smiled to herself and walked to Karisma's room as she heard her baby girl continue to giggle.

When she turned the corner and walked into the entrance of Karisma's room, the sight in front of her made her knees buckle and she felt faint. She teetered into the room slowly with her knees shaking violently and tears in her eyes. Reaching out to the side of her, her hands fell upon the top of the rocking chair where she sat to rock Karisma to sleep, and she used it to keep herself from falling over.

"L-Lloyd?" Dior called out, her voice shaking with all of the fear that she felt. She stared at the back of the familiar figure in front of her as he stood over her baby's crib, looking down. She prayed to God that it wasn't who she thought it was, but she knew that her prayers were in vain. She'd spent over ten years with Lloyd and she could tell his physique from any man on Earth.

Slowly, Lloyd turned around and Dior almost fell over when she saw that in his arms, he was cradling her baby girl. She tore her eyes away from his arms and looked into his eyes, pleading with him for mercy. She prayed that he wouldn't do anything to her child. Their child.

"So you been fuckin' this nigga longer than I thought," Lloyd said to her. His eyes pierced into hers as he spoke his venomous words with anger and the subtle hint of hurt in his voice.

"W-what are you talkin' about?" Dior asked him, sincerely confused as she looked back and forth between his face and Karisma, who was in his arms still smiling at her father.

"This fuckin' baby...this is Kenyon's fuckin' baby. You think I'm stupid?" Lloyd started.

"L-Lloyd...no! She is not his baby. She's yours!" Dior stuttered. She felt her throat closing up from the fear that was gripping her body. Her breathing was coming in short spurts and her heart was thumping in her chest so hard that it was making it even harder for her shaky legs to continue to support her.

"You think I'm stupid, Dior?! Look at her fuckin' eyes! She got that nigga's eyes! You been fuckin' him for a long time. So you two been planning this shit for a minute, huh? Set me up and get rid of me so you can have the perfect muthafuckin' family while I'm doing a lifetime bid, huh?" Lloyd accused her with narrow eyes as he walked closer to her.

Dior wanted to back away but her eyes were on her baby and she was worried for her child's life. She gripped so hard on the top of the rocking chair that her knuckles were white. With a trembling bottom lip, she opened her mouth once more to explain to Lloyd the truth.

"K-Kenyon is your c-c-cousin, Lloyd! Those eyes run in your family! I swear she's your baby! I swear!"

Lloyd stared at her with hurt in his eyes and then in a matter of a few seconds, it all went away and his face went totally stone cold. At that point, Dior knew it was over. She'd seen this expression time and time again and it always meant bad news for the person on the other end of his stare. She felt like her entire world was fading away around her. Dior saw spots in front of her eyes as she began to go faint.

"Russ and Murder, get in here and grab this bitch," Lloyd commanded with an even tone.

He said it like it was nothing. There was absolutely no emotion in his voice and Dior knew that anything he may have felt for her when he walked in the house was no longer there. Suddenly, two sets of large, rough hands grabbed onto Dior and lifted her straight off the floor. She was shivering so violently, they had to hold on to her tightly just to be able to keep her steady.

"Let's go to the kitchen," Lloyd told them.

Dior eyes opened wide and she turned to look at him and her daughter, but the men moved so quickly to obey Lloyd's command that she didn't even get a chance to turn her head before they were walking her down the hall and down the stairs. Behind her, she could hear Lloyd ranting about how her and Kenyon must have thought he was stupid or some shit. She wanted so badly to tell him 'no, they didn't' but her words were caught up in her throat and her fear wouldn't allow them to come out.

"Strap her down to a chair," Lloyd said.

Dior watched in horror as he held Karisma, who was now crying loudly as the men sat her down roughly in one of chairs at the dining room table and took out wire to strap her down. The wire pierced through her flesh as they wrapped it around her body tightly but she didn't care. The only thing she could focus on was her daughter.

"L-L-Lloyd, pleeease listen to me! She is yours! I s-s-swear!" she pleaded to him as he stood in front of her inspecting the men's work.

"You think I give a fuck about the word of a backstabbing ass bitch?" he bellowed at her. "Where the fuck is that nigga at with his rat ass?"

Dior started to cry so heavily that she couldn't see a thing. There was nothing she could do. Lloyd was going to kill her and her baby for the sins that she'd committed and there wasn't a thing she could do to stop him.

"I don't know!" she wailed out to the top of her lungs. "He left! I don't know where he is!"

"I fuckin' loved you, Dior!" Lloyd yelled at her and Dior, though she couldn't see him, thought that she could hear the hurt in his voice. "I fuckin' loved you and this is how you do me? So what a nigga fuck around from time to time? That's what niggas do! I ain't never done shit else to you!"

Dior stopped crying as she stared down at her thighs with her arms bound behind her. She could hear the shuffling of the men next to her. They were probably caught off guard at Lloyd speaking with so much pain and passion. It was something that they weren't used to. Not only that, but they knew Dior. She'd been around since the beginning. They knew that she was about to die and they hoped they weren't gonna have to be the ones to do it.

"So this is what I'mma do," Lloyd said finally. Dior rose her head up to look at him. "I'mma make this shit fast for you. I won't make you suffer."

Dior sniffled as she stared at him. She wasn't surprised. She knew when she first saw Lloyd that she was a dead woman walking. There wasn't a doubt in her mind that she wasn't going to see another day.

Lloyd turned around and hit a few buttons on the oven to turn it on. The oven chimed as it began to heat up and she heard the sound of the gas from inside of it when it turned on. Dior crinkled her brows in fear and confusion as she watched Lloyd. He opened the oven door and to her absolute dismay, he did the most horrifying thing that she could have ever possibly fathomed him doing. He placed her crying child inside.

"Oh my God! Noooo, please Lloyd! Don't hurt her! She's your child! PLEASE!!!"

Dior began bucking and kicking in the chair so hard that it toppled over and she landed with a loud thud on her side. Her head hit the edge of the table on the way down but the stinging pain in her head didn't faze her in the least. The terror that she felt over her child being placed in a heated oven, overshadowed anything else she could think or feel.

As she yelled out for mercy, she became aware of Lloyd's presence above her head. Her cries and pleas became murmurs and babbling of words that made no sense. She felt herself going mad in her last moments as she thought of her child. There was nothing she could do to save her.

"Remember this as you burn in hell. For every action, there is a reaction. When you shit on the ones who love you, the shit comes back. If you not strong enough to take the consequences, you shouldn't play the fuckin' game. Goodnight, Dior," Lloyd said.

Pow!

FIFTEEN

"HEY!" Tish exclaimed when Keisha walked in the house.

Keisha muttered her greeting and then threw her purse on the counter and walked to the fridge to pour herself a drink. It needed to be something strong. Just her luck, the strongest thing she saw in there was a Sprite. For two bartenders, you would think their fridge would be stocked full of liquor but, of course, it wasn't.

"Shit, we don't have anything to drink?" Keisha asked as she sat down on a barstool. When she turned and focused her eyes on Tish for the first time since she'd walked in their apartment, she noticed that Tish was holding a large bottle of Cîroc in one hand and a small glass in the other.

Bingo!

Without saying anything, Keisha was about to reach out for the bottle when she took a second glance at Tish. She was wearing a short, thin lace robe that was so small, it didn't close all the way at the top and her large bosoms were propped up and on full display. The robe was see-through so Keisha could also see that Tish wasn't wearing anything underneath but a thin, pink thong and a teeny, sequined matching bra. When Keisha dropped her head to Tish's feet, she saw that she was wearing stiletto heels.

"Um...you expecting someone?" Keisha asked her as she took another look up and down at Tish's attire.

"No..." Tish said slowly. Something about her tone seemed off but Keisha dismissed it thinking that maybe Tish was embarrassed about what she was wearing. "Anyways, let's not talk about that. What are you doin' here? I thought you planned on spending the day with Trigga...I mean, isn't that what you said in your text?"

Keisha sighed and grabbed the glass and bottle of Cîroc from Tish then poured herself a full glass before speaking. She didn't bother mixing it with anything else, she planned on sipping it straight. With the day she'd had and the life she was living, she could use it.

"Well, I did but Trigga was arrested...for a double homicide."

Keisha put the glass to her lips and gulped down half the clear liquid inside as Tish gawked at her. Her mouth was moving and her eyes were wide but no sound was coming out. Finally, Tish found her voice and spoke.

"*Double* homicide?!" Tish whispered. Keisha scrunched up her face at her friend. Why was she whispering?

"Yep, double. They said some homeless couple was found dead in his hotel room last night. Someone killed them and they think he had something to do with it."

Tish's mouth was hanging wide open. "But wasn't he with you last night?"

Keisha nodded her head and took another gulp. "Part of it. I fell asleep and he was in the bed. When I woke up early this morning, he was sleeping on the sofa. Who knows? Maybe he did have something to do with it. I mean, what do I really know about this guy? I told him that I loved him and if you really think about it, I don't know *a thing…*"

"YOU TOLD HIM THAT YOU LOVED HIM?!" Tish shrieked then covered her mouth with her hand and turned back towards her room. Keisha frowned again.

"What is wrong with you?"

"Don't worry about it. Now wait…you told him you loved him?" Keisha nodded. "Keesh, I told you this guy is bad news. Look at what has happened to you since you met him. Now he's been arrested for *murder*!"

Feeling the buzz, Keisha nodded her head again as she listened to Tish. She was right. Keisha didn't know much about him but when it came to him, for some reason it didn't matter. What she did know was enough to make her feelings for him strong.

"Listen to me," Tish said. She grabbed onto Keisha's chin and held her head steady, making her look her in the eyes. "You have to leave him alone. He's not the one for you. He's sexy and all, but he's another Lloyd. He's a street nigga. And from what I've seen, he's nothing but trouble. Just look at your fuckin' life and tell me I'm wrong!"

Keisha felt like crying again and it pissed her off when she realized it. She was so tired of the crybaby she was becoming. But she'd only become this way recently, since she'd met Trigga. Before him, she'd been in the process of getting her life on track. She had been in school, she had a job, and had gotten her own place. Shit wasn't perfect but it damn sure wasn't bad either. And she didn't wake up and go to bed every day afraid that the day might be her last.

"You're right," Keisha admitted. "I—"

"Tee-baby, what's taking you so long?" a voice said from behind.

Keisha frowned at the voice she was hearing for two reasons. The first reason was that it sounded familiar to her. She knew the voice of the speaker although she couldn't quite place it. The second reason for her frown, the more shocking reason, was that the voice was female.

Swiveling on the barstool, Keisha tore her eyes away from the sheepish and embarrassed expression on Tish's face and looked into the face of the speaker. A smile crossed her face when she focused in on who it was.

"Luxe?" Keisha said but it wasn't a question.

She turned around to look at Tish who had her elbows rested on the countertop and was running her hand over her face as if she were stressed.

"Lauren, damn. I told you to wait for me in the room," Tish reminded her with a sigh.

"I know," Luxe responded with a soft pout on her face. "But you had me waiting too long."

She walked over to where Tish was and ran her fingers done her spine in a sexy manner as she looked at Keisha in a way that made her believe that Luxe knew exactly what she was doing by coming out of the room when she heard Keisha's voice, wearing nothing but a small half tank-top and a gold thong. Her long hair was pushed to one side and was ruffled so it looked messy, like she'd spent all morning rolling around in the bed.

Keisha shot Tish a sneaky grin and then drained the last of the Cîroc in her glass. She'd never questioned the fact that she'd never seen Tish bring home a guy since they'd been living together. She figured it wasn't her business. She'd seen her talk to and flirt with guys at the club, but it never went anywhere and Keisha never thought anything of it. Now she knew why.

"Well, I'm going to go to my room," Keisha told them as she twisted around and hopped off the barstool. "You two have fun. Tish, I'll talk to you later on."

"Yeah, yeah, yeah," Tish groaned. Then turning to Luxe, she said, "Get your jealous ass in the room. I told you she don't swing this way!"

Covering her mouth with her hand, Keisha stifled a giggle and walked into her room. Without bothering to take off her shoes, she belly-flopped on her bed and instantly her worries came back to her mind. As she heard Tish and Luxe walk into the room and close the door, Trigga's words replayed over and over again in her mind.

Lloyd was out of jail. He had done so much wicked stuff in his life, how was it that he could possibly escape prison after a mere few weeks? She hadn't thought it would be possible.

Sitting up, Keisha reached over and opened the drawer that she'd stashed Trigga's gun. When she picked it up, she held the heavy, cold steel in the palm of her hand and juggled the weight over her fingers. She replayed in her mind what Trigga had said when he gave it to her.

"Click this button to turn off the safety before pulling the trigger. There is already one in the chamber. All you have to do is turn off the safety, then aim and shoot. Got it?"

Exhaling heavily, Keisha reached over and stuffed the gun back in the dresser. She started to close the drawer and then stopped suddenly when her eyes fell upon the drugs that she had placed in there; the pills and coke that she'd taken from Lloyd's condo before she left. She grabbed one of the bags of coke and pulled it out.

All noise faded away from around her as she held it in her hand and stared at it. Her mind was telling her 'no' but her body was telling her 'yes'; she needed it…just a small hit to get over the stress of the day. To go from being at the happiest point, wrapped in Trigga's arms, to the worst point when she had to watch him being taken away in handcuffs, was a lot for her. And now, she wanted to confide in Tish, she wanted to tell her friend about everything while crying and sipping on drinks or shoveling ice cream in her mouth, but she couldn't because Tish was preoccupied with Luxe.

After debating for a few minutes within the confines of her mind, Keisha halted the debate when she arrived on a clear decision. She dumped the powder onto the top of her dark cherry oak nightstand and used a business card on the table to cut it into three straight lines. She leaned down to take in the first line and the anticipation of it all made her heart beat fast. Her mouth watered as she thought about the feeling of ecstasy and relaxation that overcame her when she was in that numb state that made all of her problems fade away.

Then her phone rang.

Keisha closed her eyes and cursed under her breath at the sound of her iPhone sounding off on the bed behind her. She turned around to silence it but something stopped her. It was an 800 number but for some reason, she felt compelled to answer it.

"Hello?" Keisha answered. She glanced over at the lines of coke on her nightstand and then bit her lip as a feeling of guilt washed over her. "Hello?"

Pulling the phone away from her face, she looked at the screen and noticed that the line had gone dead. She frowned and then pressed the button to redial the number.

"If you received a call from this number, it means you received a call from an inmate at…"

Keisha's lips parted into an 'o' shape as she listened. Trigga had tried to call her and she'd missed it. She'd missed it because she'd been about to snort a line of coke. She hung up the phone and grabbed her laptop to check whether he was on the jail's website so that she could get information on him. After searching for about twenty minutes, she wasn't able to find a thing. Nothing in the news, nothing on the jail's site…nothing.

Keisha glanced over at the lines on her nightstand and shook her head. She couldn't snort them now. It just didn't feel right. So instead she closed her eyes and forced herself to go to sleep, by clearing her thoughts of all the happenings of the day and returning back to the moments of earlier. The moments that she'd spent in perfect peace with Trigga.

SIXTEEN

"The fuck you doin'? You only get one call!" the greasy, pale white jailer blubbered at Trigga as he narrowed his eyes at him.

"There was no answer," Trigga said between clenched teeth.

The man crossed his arms in front of him and frowned deeply as he glared at Trigga. Trigga kept his face blank but his eyes remained fixated on the guard's face as he waited for him to either pose a problem or let him be.

"Okay, you get one more call but I'm watchin' your ass!"

Trigga didn't respond, he only turned towards the phone and thought hard about what he was going to do. He wanted to call Keisha back but she'd already not answered once. What if she didn't answer again? He didn't want to risk it.

Closing his eyes, he prayed that his photographic memory would come to his aid when he needed it most. Thinking back to the number that had flashed across his phone screen that morning, Trigga keyed in the ten digits and waited on the line.

"Um...hello?"

"It's me...Trigga."

LEO SULLIVAN & PORSCHA STERLING

"Trigga!" the voice on the other end exclaimed. "Hey, what number is this that you're calling me from?"

Trigga shot a look at the guard who was watching him so closely, he could probably see Trigga's words forming in his brain before he even spoke them.

"Tasha, I need you to help me out with something. I'm in jail—"

"WHAT?!" Tasha yelled out. "Oh my GOD! Is it because of the guard at the coffee shop? Did you go back there? Trigga, why would you—"

"TASHA!" Trigga snapped. He eyed the guard who had jumped and moved towards him at the sound of his raised voice. Gritting his teeth together, he continued a tad quieter. "Tasha, it's not about the guard. I don't know how much it will be to bail me out but I promise if you're able to get it some way to bail me out, I'll pay you back extra. If you can't, don't worry. I will figure something else out."

"Okay," Tasha said so quickly that it almost threw Trigga off how fast she responded and how calm she was. She was a good, innocent college student. For her to agree so quickly and to all of a sudden be so calm about it, struck him as odd but he was grateful for her reaction.

"My government is Maurice Bivens. I should be going in front of the judge in the morning for first appearance and he'll set the bail amount so—"

"Don't worry, Trigga. I got it. I know how it works," she said. Trigga's eyebrow lifted up at that. How could she possibly know how it worked?

"Hey, time's up, pretty boy," the guard said as he moved towards Trigga.

Trigga shot him a menacing look that stopped him in his tracks and made him grab on to the baton at his waist.

"I'll talk to you soon, Tasha. I'm sorry for callin' like this but I appreciate it."

"I got your back," she said back to him and, despite his situation, it made him smile a little.

"I said time's up, smiley. Hang it up before I do it for you!" the guard bellowed from behind Trigga.

Without saying goodbye, Trigga placed the phone down and clamped his mouth shut to keep himself from going off on the fat ass guard who was nearly breathing down his neck. All he could do was pray hard that Tasha was able to get him out of jail the next day because if he had to stay any longer, he wasn't sure he'd be able to make it without killing somebody.

SEVENTEEN

Kenyon pulled up to his house and immediately knew that something wasn't right. The front door was wide open and Dior was nowhere to be found. Dior wasn't a super paranoid person but she wasn't one to leave the door wide open. She also was the type to flip the fuck out if she even saw a small ass spider, so it struck Kenyon as odd that she would leave the door that way.

Upon further inspection, he saw a dark-colored, unmarked car situated a few houses down from the house, but he saw there was a driver inside who had a clear view of the house. Kenyon stopped his car suddenly and squinted into the car. He recognized the man. He was the same dude he'd seen outside the police precinct that one day.

Kenyon jumped out the car and crept over to the man who seemed to be texting someone on his phone. When he got close enough to the vehicle, he pulled out his pistol which had a silencer already attached and fired a shot right into the man's skull. The driver slumped over into the passenger seat immediately. Grabbing the car door, Kenyon cranked up the car, rolled up the window and then turned off the engine. After he checked on Dior and Karisma, he and his family would be out of the city as soon as possible, way before the man's body began stinking and a neighbor called the cops.

"Dior!" Kenyon yelled as he walked into the house.

She didn't answer back. Something was terribly wrong and with every step he took into the house, fear began to set in to his body. If something happened to Dior and the baby while he was gone, he'd never forgive himself.

Then just as he was about to run upstairs to try to find Dior, he heard the sound of muffled crying. It was Karisma and it seemed to be coming from the kitchen. Kenyon took off in a mad dash towards the kitchen, holding his breath the entire time. He didn't even realize that he wasn't breathing until he walked around the corner into the kitchen and ran right into Dior's bloody body.

"DIOR! NOOOO!" Kenyon yelled as he grabbed her by her neck and tried to raise her head up. Her eyes were closed and he couldn't feel a pulse but he wasn't sure if it was because there wasn't one or because his own heart was beating so hard in his chest. There was blood everywhere.

The crying continued and it pulled his attention away from the bloody body in his hands.

Karisma!

Kenyon pulled himself away from Dior's body as his eyes searched vigorously around the kitchen for the source of the crying. He didn't see the baby anywhere. Then his eyes fell upon the luminescent dials on the top of the stainless steel range.

The oven!

Kenyon immediately broke out into a sweat as he dashed over to the oven and in less than a second he'd pulled the oven door open and pulled out Karisma from inside. She was warm to his touch but, thankfully, she didn't seem to be hurt. Dior had been complaining for weeks about the oven taking longer than normal to heat up, but Kenyon hadn't bothered to get it fixed because she'd barely been cooking. Adjusting to being a mother and dealing with the stress of her new life left her no time to be a homemaker, so Kenyon didn't bother rushing to get it fixed. It was a good thing.

After Kenyon took the time to inspect Karisma and make sure that she wasn't hurt, he placed her down softly on top of a small towel and ran back over to Dior. He grabbed his cell phone out of his pocket and dialed 9-1-1 while using his other hand to cut her loose. When she was loose, her bloodied body collapsed and he grabbed her with both arms, as he balanced the phone between his ear and shoulder.

"Hello, what's your emergency?"

"My girl...she got shot, I need y'all to get an ambulance out here NOW!" Kenyon yelled as he held tightly onto Dior. He fell to the floor and pulled her so that she was lying between his legs.

"Sir, is there a pulse?" the operator asked him.

"Shit...I-I-I don't know! There's so much blood...can you just send a fuckin' ambulance?!"

"Sir, we have someone on the way but I'm just trying to collect information from you. I need you to check if she has a pulse."

It wasn't until that moment that Kenyon realized he had tears spilling down his eyes. Sucking in a deep breath, he reached down and pressed his fingers against Dior's neck. He held his breath as he prayed and waited, hoping that he would feel something that would point towards her being alive.

But there was nothing.

Kenyon's soul was crushed and for the first time in his life, since he first learned of his mother's death, he cried as if there was no tomorrow. He held onto Dior's lifeless body as the phone fell from his ear onto the floor. He could hear the high-pitch voice of the operator on the other line asking him questions that he didn't have the strength to answer. His whole world was falling apart.

The one woman he'd waited so long for was gone.

EIGHTEEN

"Where are you going?"

Keisha glanced over her shoulder at Tish before walking to the kitchen and grabbing a bottled water out of the refrigerator.

"Do you really want me to tell you?" she asked her as she twisted the cap and took a sip.

"Yes, actually I do. Damn bitch, when we get so mysterious with each other?" Tish said giving her a stank look before she walked over in front of her and placed her hand on her hip. Keisha rolled her eyes.

"You should talk. How long have you and Luxe nasty ass been messing around?"

That fixed Tish's attitude. Her face fell and she blinked a few times before answering.

"Look, Keesh…it's just something I'm tryin' out for the first time—"

Keisha put her hand up to stop her. "I ain't judgin' you on that shit. It's none of my business. I just don't want no shit from you because I'm about to bail Trigga out of jail."

Tish's mouth dropped open.

"How the fuck you gonna do that? He was locked up for double homicide! That bond gotta be high as hell. Where you get the money from?"

Keisha took another swig of water and then twisted the top back on the bottle. "I got it courtesy of Lloyd."

"That's the money you stole from him? Awwwww, shit. You got a death wish. Dead bitch walkin'," Tish said. She threw her hands up in the air like Keisha was a lost cause.

"It may be stupid but I feel like it's what I gotta do," Keisha told her. She grabbed her purse and started to walk to the door but then she stopped suddenly. "Tish, if I were to move for a while, would you be okay?"

Tish gave Keisha a knowing look like it was something she'd been expecting her to say. Then she exhaled and stood up from the barstool that she'd been leaning on.

"I'll be fine. I already kinda figured something would happen…either you would move out of Atlanta because of all the shit going on here or you would move in with Trigga. I don't know, I just felt the time would come," she said somberly. Then she pepped up. "But I'm good. Luxe's lease will be up soon. Maybe she'll move in or something, who knows."

Tish turned around quickly after adding that last part like it was nothing. But Keisha wasn't going to let her just push that out like it wasn't anything and leave.

"Wait a minute! Y'all movin' kinda fast, huh?" Keisha asked Tish's back. Tish turned around and winked at her as she pulled her long hair into a ponytail.

"Kinda," she said with a smirk on her face. "But so are you."

Keisha couldn't even argue with that point. She was moving kinda fast as well. For her to only know Trigga a few months and already be considering moving to New York City with him when she'd barely ever been out of Georgia, it was a big step. But something felt right about being with him and she didn't think she would be happy if she didn't.

***

"There must be some mistake…he was just on the website this morning. Maurice Bivens and the charge is for a double homicide," Keisha said to the bails bondsmen again. She leaned over the counter and tried to look on his screen as he pecked away on the keyboard, searching for Trigga's name again.

"I know he was on here. I'm the one who spoke to you on the phone. But what I'm trying to say to you is that he's not on here now. Someone paid for him to get out," the man informed her, as he frowned and pulled on the edge of his monitor to stop her from being able to see his screen.

"Well, is he out already?" Keisha asked with her hand on her hip. Then she ran her fingers through her short hair and reached in her purse for her cell phone. If he was out, maybe she could give him a call to see if everything was okay.

He adjusted his glasses on his chestnut brown face and rubbed his long beard as he stared at her and shrugged.

"He could be. The jail is right down the street from here so you can go check with them."

Keisha turned on her heels and walked out before the bondsmen could finish his sentence. She knew that he really didn't want to go out of his way to help her. He saw her as another poor, pitiful woman who was in love with a future felon and would spend her life holding on to her sex in hopes that one day her man would meet her again on the outside. Maybe that was her and maybe she was being stupid by still trying to be with Trigga but she'd find out when she got to that point.

Only about five minutes later, Keisha pulled up in front of the jail and then slowed to a stop as she searched for a place to park. There was a parking garage nearby that she saw when she first pulled up but she didn't see herself paying ten dollars for five minutes even if she could afford it.

"Shit...there ain't no damn curb I can park up on?" Keisha cursed as she crept up slowly in front of the jail.

Then suddenly her eyes fell upon a familiar figure to the side of her standing in front of the jail.

That can't be who I think it is, Keisha thought to herself. *Tasha?*

She rolled down the window so she could call out to her friend from class, the one who had been sending her over her notes from the classes they shared for the past week, but she was cut off when she saw another person join her outside on the steps of the jail.

"Trigga?" Keisha said as she squinted out the window.

Keisha watched with her mouth wide open as she saw Trigga walk out with a huge smile on his face. When he caught up to Tasha, he reached out and pulled her into a one-armed hug and kissed her gently on her cheek. Tasha blushed so hard that, although her skin was a dark chocolate, it was almost like you could still see it. She pushed her curly 'fro out of her face as the wind blew her long tresses in every direction, while she and Trigga walked away happily. Tasha reached out to grab Trigga's hand and he hesitated for a moment as if thinking on something, but he shrugged and took it anyways.

Keisha tried to continue to watch them but the tears that rose up in her eyes stopped her from being able to see their images. She felt an empty feeling in her stomach as Trigga and Tasha walked happily hand in hand. It was a gut-wrenching feeling. She felt more alone in that moment than she'd ever had in her entire life.

NINETEEN

"Oh my God! Keisha, is that you?" Tasha called out suddenly. "What are you doing here?"

Alarmed, Keisha jumped in her seat at the sound of Tasha's voice. She'd been so caught up in her own feelings of dread and betrayal that she hadn't even realized the moment that Tasha had turned towards her. The tears finally fell from Keisha's eyes, clearing her vision, and she wiped them away quickly and took a deep breath.

Forcing a smile on her face, she looked out the window at Tasha and Trigga. Once Trigga's eyes fell on her, he pulled away from Tasha and his mouth dropped open suddenly. He looked extremely uncomfortable and Keisha could see it. Tasha noticed it, too.

"Hey Tasha, I'm here doing what you're doing. Coming to pick up a nigga who ain't worth shit," Keisha said with a forced smile. Tasha's face dropped suddenly and she frowned before looking over at Trigga who was walking at a fast pace towards the car, which was actually his car.

"Keesh! What the—"

"Wait," Tasha started. The smile that had seconds ago been so deeply etched in her face, disappeared immediately as she looked back and forth between Trigga and Keisha. "You two know each other?"

"Know each other? Yes, we do," Keisha started.

Grabbing her purse, she jumped out the car and walked over to where Trigga and Tasha stood. Trigga tried to reach out for her but she backed away, yet she didn't miss the hurt that passed through Tasha's eyes when she saw his gesture.

"Matter of fact, just *yesterday* morning you were tellin' me you loved me, weren't you?" Keisha asked as she looked at Trigga.

People were starting to stare from around the front of the building and even some nosey ass people from inside were walking out, as Keisha stood with her hands on her hips and glared at Trigga. She felt like she was once again at the same place that Lloyd had placed her months ago when she found out that not only was he not planning on divorcing Dior, but that she was also pregnant. Once again, Keisha found out that she was the side chick, hopelessly in love with a man who didn't really give a fuck about her.

"Keisha, give me a minute to—"

"You told her you loved her?" Tasha piped up. Keisha turned to look at her with wide eyes, it was almost as if she had forgotten that she was there for a minute.

"You said that you *loved* her?" Tasha repeated. She had tears in her eyes and her voice was cracking as she spoke. "You just took my virginity a couple days ago! I GAVE YOU MY VIRGINITY and the next day you were with her?"

Keisha's mouth dropped open at Tasha's revelation. A few people standing around them gasped and one person even yelled out 'oh, shit!' as they watched the drama unfolding around them.

"Wait a minute, Tash…you ain't my chick and all I wanted to do was fuck. You ain't tell me shit about you being a virgin," Trigga said through clenched teeth.

This situation was exactly what he didn't want to be in and that's why he'd made it his business not to get caught up with females to wherein they caught feelings.

"How could you do this to me? I just used my college tuition to bail you out of jail!"

Tasha broke out in loud sobs and dropped her head in her hands, as Keisha stared at her like she almost wanted to have pity for her. Before his very eyes, Keisha walked over and grabbed Tasha into a hug and started patting her on the back.

"Shhhh, stop cryin'," Keisha told her quietly. "That muthafucka ain't worth it." She shot a look at Trigga that pissed him the fuck off.

"Man, Keesh, stop with this silly shit and get your ass in the car. Tasha, I told you I would give you your money back as soon as I get out, so you can stop that fuckin' cryin'," he gritted.

"I'm not gettin' in no damn car wit' yo' ass! You played me!" Keisha yelled out. Out the corner of her eye, she saw two uniformed police officers walking slowly towards them. They had smiles on their faces as if they were enjoying the show and were in no hurry to break it up.

"Ain't nobody play yo' ass! I called you first to bail me out and you ain't answer so I asked Tasha. I ain't plan on callin' her ass for shit ever again, until I needed to get the fuck outta jail so I could check up on you!" Tasha began to wail louder at Trigga's words and Keisha backed away from her, slowly releasing her from her embrace.

"And yes, I fucked but I ain't know shit about her being no virgin! Now, I'm sorry about that shit, but a nigga wanted to fuck and I didn't want to make no moves on you until you was ready!" Trigga turned to Tasha and glared at her as she continued to sob loudly as if it were the end of the world. "And for a fuckin' virgin, she was offerin' up the pussy like a pro so I took it. Damn!"

Trigga stuffed his hands in his pockets and frowned at the small crowd of onlookers around them. Then he turned around and came eye-to-eye with the police who were approaching them. He was frustrated to the max but, even in the midst of being hurt by him, Keisha still found the way that he stood tall and agitated in the center of the crowd, so damn sexy. She almost hated herself for it. It was like she was returning to the weak, whipped, low self-esteem woman that Lloyd had turned her into years ago.

"Keesh, just get in the fuckin' car and let's go. I'll take you home."

Keisha looked at the crowd around her. All of the people were staring at her with their eyes wide as they waited to see what she would do. Then her eyes dropped and she focused on Tasha, her friend, who was severely hurt by Trigga's action. Then it dawned on her. She wasn't herself in this new love triangle. She was Dior and Tasha was her. Tasha was the one used and Dior was the one who Lloyd fucked around on and she just stayed there and took it. Did she really want to lead the life Dior led?

Difference is, Trigga is not your husband. Shit, he ain't even your man! Keisha screamed out to herself in her thoughts.

And they were right. She couldn't be mad at him over something that they hadn't even discussed. She didn't even know where she stood in Trigga's life. She knew what he'd said to her the other day, but it was really her fault for staking claim on a man who wasn't hers to begin with.

"You know what? You're absolutely right. Tasha isn't your girl and neither am I. I forgot that simple fact," Keisha said in a low tone. She crossed her arms in front of her chest and nodded her head at Trigga. "You're in the right."

Trigga gawked at her for a few minutes like she had lost her mind. Then he came forward and grabbed her by her arm and pushed her towards his Porsche. "Man, shut that crazy shit up and get your loony ass in the car. You are my muthafuckin' girl. The fuck you thinkin', Keesh?"

Keisha felt the flutters in her stomach when he came near her. Yeah, she was in the middle of another fucked up situation but this was different from what went down with her and Lloyd. And the way that Trigga grabbed her and pulled her to the passenger side of the SUV before opening the door and helping her in gently, while still donning the deep frown that he had on his face, was sexy to her. He was in complete control and, no matter how bad she felt about Tasha, he made sure Keisha knew that she was the one he wanted. Tasha was just an unfortunate situation.

"Listen Tasha," Keisha heard Trigga say. "I'll pay you back for what you did in there…plus interest, because I appreciate you lookin' out. But you came at me wit' sex so I took dat shit. I ain't kno' you was no virgin and you knew dat when I hit it. I'll call you later on today so we can meet up and you can get your money back."

"No need!" Keisha yelled out the window. She reached in her purse and pulled out the envelope of cash that she had in there and held it out to Trigga. "Pay her ass back right now!"

Trigga grabbed the envelope and gave Keisha a look as if to ask where in the world she got all that cash from. She shrugged and crossed her arms in front of her chest as she watched him and Tasha intently. Tasha had finally stood up and looked an absolute mess. Her mascara was smudged all over her face and her eyes were red and puffy. She didn't look sad anymore, however, she looked angry.

Trigga counted out the money in the envelope and handed it all to her before checking his surroundings. Most of the crowd had disappeared as soon as the ratchetness had come to a halt once Keisha was back in the car.

"Take your ass straight to your car before you get mugged or some shit out here," Trigga warned her as he pushed the envelope in her hands.

Tasha took it and pressed it against her chest, but her eyes narrowed in on Keisha as Trigga walked away. Keisha pushed her nose in the air and looked away. There wasn't anything she could say to the girl. Yeah, she had liked her but she couldn't help the coincidence that occurred between them today. They could no longer be friends anymore. Those days were over.

"I would have thought after playing side bitch to Lloyd you would have learned to stop fuckin' around with no good thug niggas, Keisha. I guess I was wrong about you," Tasha sneered. Her words were said so maliciously, it almost felt like they cut straight through Keisha.

Keisha's mouth fell open as she stared at Tasha, but it wasn't even because of the fact that the words she said hurt. It was because of the fact that Tasha's words made Trigga stop dead in his tracks. He was standing in front of the Porsche and his back was to Tasha but even while looking at his side profile, Keisha could tell from the stricken look on his face that he'd heard her every word.

"Yeah, you got dirty laundry, too! You wanna sit all high and mighty in there like you won, but not too long ago you were in my position…playing side bitch to Lloyd while he went home at night to lay next to his pregnant wife, Dior!"

In two seconds, Keisha had bolted from the car and was on top of Tasha beating the shit out of her.

TWENTY

Trigga stood for a few seconds and watched the women, as they fell to the street with punches flying and hair pulling all over the place. He knew he had to hurry up and break it up before the police ran back outside, but part of him wanted to just chuck the deuces at them both and drive off.

Did she say that Keisha was playing side bitch to Lloyd? Trigga thought to himself.

At first he thought there was no way in hell he was hearing right but when Tasha mentioned Lloyd's pregnant wife, Dior, Trigga knew she was talking about the same man. Tasha was right, Keisha did have her own secrets because all the time they'd spent together not once did she mention that she knew Lloyd. He'd been blaming himself for bringing her into shit that had nothing to do with her, and now he was finding out that she was in it from jump. Matter of fact, she might be the reason for all the shit that was happening.

"BITCH!" Keisha yelled as she grabbed a chunk of Tasha's natural hair and yanked hard, so hard that Tasha started bleeding from the scalp and let out a shrill scream. Once again, the crowd had returned to watch the hoe-down they'd wanted to see earlier.

"Shit," Trigga muttered under his breath. He was mad as hell at the shit that Tasha had just let him in on earlier, but he knew he wouldn't be able to get to the bottom of it with Keisha in jail for assault.

Walking over, he ducked and dodged the punches flying back and forth and grabbed Keisha up around her waist, lifting her clear off the ground. She continued to punch and kick at Tasha, so he shook the shit out of her to make her stop.

"Man, get your ass in the car," Trigga said through his teeth.

The way he said it made Keisha stop fighting instantly. He placed her down on her feet and she took one last look at Tasha who was shooting daggers at her through her eyes, then jumped into the passenger side of the SUV. Before Keisha could even put on her seatbelt, Trigga took off from the jail at top speed, cutting off some drivers who angrily punched their horn as he drove away.

"Trigga, me and Lloyd…it was just—"

"Don't even open your fuckin' mouth to tell that lie," Trigga snapped at her in a rough tone that she'd never heard from him before.

Keisha's eyes widened as she looked at him. All the care that he'd had in his face for her earlier was gone. In its place was a blank, emotionless stare. They drove down the road in silence at high speed, as Trigga dodged and dipped in front of other cars. He cut a twenty minute trip down to ten minutes and before Keisha knew it, she was in front of her apartment.

"Get out," was all Trigga said to her.

When he said the words, he flinched with guilt so subtly that he knew she couldn't have seen it. It hurt him to speak to her that way but he couldn't help but feel that he'd been so stupid and so wrong about her. Money Over Bitches, it was the motto that had gotten him so far. And now he'd fallen victim to a woman who had turned his world upside down. How could he even be sure that Mase wasn't trying to kill him over some shit that she'd planted in his head, the same way she planted it in his? She could have been working with Lloyd all along, playing the two of them against each other so that, in the end, Lloyd could kill them both and be the ultimate victor.

"Trigga, I understand that you're upset but it's not what you think. I'm not working with Lloyd," Keisha said to him sadly.

Her voice cracked as she spoke because she knew that there wasn't a thing she could say to get Trigga to believe her. He would have to just take her at her word and right now her word didn't mean shit. She should have told him what was up with her and Lloyd before he found out from someone else. The fact that she'd hidden that from him for so long just made everything worse.

"Okay, and why should I believe that, Keesh?" Trigga asked her with his head down. A glimmer of hope went through Keisha's body. She could tell that Trigga wanted to believe her. He was torn in between going with his mind or going with his heart.

"Because I love you and I swear that I'm not doing anything with Lloyd. I swear that I haven't been lying to you. If I was working with him, wouldn't you already be dead?"

She had a point and Trigga knew it. In his heart of hearts, he didn't feel like Keisha would pull some shady shit on him like that. Not to mention the fact that she was laid up in the hospital at the same time he had been. Both of them had been fighting for their lives while the two who were working together, Mase and Lloyd, were just fine. It didn't add up that she would be with Lloyd still.

Without saying a word, Trigga got out of the car and walked over to Keisha's side. He grabbed the handle and opened the door then reached out his hand for the key she was holding in her hands. She frowned at him and handed it to him silently. Trigga put his index finger in the air as if telling her to 'hold on' then walked to her door and unlocked it. After pushing it open, he walked back to where she sat with an inquisitive stare, waiting to see what he was up to. Trigga reached into her side of the car, and scooped her up easily within his arms as if she weighed only one pound and walked her into the apartment, kicking the door closed behind him.

Tish walked out of her room holding her purse and keys in her hand, almost at the exact time that Keisha and Trigga rounded the corner into her bedroom.

"Well, damn! Y'all have the place to yourselves! I'm outta here," she told them.

Keisha laughed a little to herself but it was nervous laughter, because she still wasn't completely sure what Trigga had planned.

He kicked her room door closed behind them, and placed her on the bed gently. The lights were off in the room and her blinds were closed so the room was dark, but Keisha could see him as he took off his clothes quickly. Then, he reached over and started unbuckling her jeans and tugged them off her curvy, thin frame. She lifted her hips in the air to help him, still unsure of exactly what was going on. It was obvious to her that sex was about to happen but Trigga hadn't responded to their argument from earlier. Did he believe her or was this their last moment?

Trigga wasted no time answering her question. Leaning down, he positioned his long pole right at the entrance of her moist cave and then put his lips right next to her ear.

"I love you, Keisha."

And the next feeling that Keisha felt after his cool breath hit her ear, was him slamming all twelve inches of his thickness right into her. Keisha bit down hard on her lip as she tried to hold in her screams of painful pleasure, but when she heard the front door close and knew for a fact that Tish was out, she stopped holding it in and let it all out. Not only were the neighbors gonna know his name, the whole damn block would too.

When it seemed like she was about to reach her climax, Trigga pulled out and grabbed her by her leg, then flipped her so she was on her stomach. He pressed down on her back to perfect her arch and then dove right in again. Keisha grinded her teeth together and fought to keep her arch right, but she was about two seconds from pushing Trigga away because she could feel him all up in her gut.

"GOTDAAAAMN IT, TRIGGAAAA!" Keisha yelled out.

She tried to scoot away but Trigga grabbed her around her waist and pulled her ass right back, then continued to clamp down on her tightly to stop her from moving. She didn't know if she was grateful for him holding her in place or if she wanted to cuss his ass out for it. Either way, the sensation of pain-mixed-pleasure was so good that he had all her emotions fucked up. She wanted to beg him for more and punch his ass for being so rough, all at the same damn time.

Gritting her teeth and tearing all the shit off the bed was the only thing that she could do when she felt herself about to cum. The movement in and out was driving Keisha insane but when he started to throw that dick in a circle, she couldn't take it any longer.

"FUUUUUUCK!" Keisha yelled out as she squeezed her toes and brought her ass up higher in the air. Trigga grabbed her up under her stomach, right where she was bended at and stroked long and hard into her hole like he knew she was about to cum. Then finally, he reached his hand under her and played with her nub with his thumb, while he popped his other thumb in her ass. That sent her wild. There was no holding back and within in a matter of seconds, she'd creamed all over her dick and the only thing you could hear other than her moans of pleasure was the smacking sound of wet skin-on-skin.

"This pussy so wet for me, Keesh," Trigga moaned as he continued working her insides. "How you get so wet for me?"

"I'm always wet for you, daddy," Keisha purred as she squeezed her eyes shut and contracted her muscles, making her pussy grip him.

"Oh shit!" Trigga moaned, throwing his head back as he enjoyed the feeling. "Shit, you know how to grip this dick just right. You nasty as fuck…shit!"

Keisha felt him stiffen up and she knew he was only seconds away from cumming so she tightened up her muscles even more.

"Cum inside me, baby," she heard herself coo as she threw her tight pussy back on him. "Cum for me."

Trigga didn't even make her wait. Within seconds of her command, he obliged and shot off what felt like a bucket load of his juice right into her. They collapsed onto the bed, Trigga butt-naked and Keisha wearing only her t-shirt, and they fell asleep in each other's arms.

TWENTY-ONE

Trigga awoke to the sound of muffled screams and water splashing on his face. Blinking his eyes at a fast-pace, he jumped when he realized he wasn't in a dream and instinctually reached out for his Glock 9. But then he remembered that the police had confiscated it. He'd made a mental note to ask Keisha to give him back the one he gave to her but when they got to her spot, he had more important shit on his mind and forgot. Now he wished he hadn't.

"Rise and shine, Trigga," a voice said from above him.

Trigga peered out in front of him but all he could see were shadows. He reached out to his side to feel for Keisha, but there was an empty spot where she'd been. He felt his chest tighten up and he sat up on the bed, careful not to make any sudden movements. He knew who the voice belonged to and he hoped like hell that Keisha was okay.

The light in the room flicked on and Trigga blinked a few times, as his eyes adjusted to the light. He didn't make any sudden movements, not because he was afraid but because he didn't know what was going on with Keisha yet and he needed to make sure that before anything, she was okay.

"You haven't been answering my calls," the icy voice said from above him.

Trigga clenched his jaw as he looked above at the figure in front of him. He wasn't afraid but he was definitely pissed off. True, he had been given a job that he was supposed to be doing and so far he'd taking the long route when it came to getting it done, but the last thing he needed was for 'mother hen' to come checking in on him..

"I was…detained for a minute," Trigga said through his teeth as he looked in Queen's light brown eyes. "

She stood tall in front of him with only a medium-length, beautiful floral dress on. The red hues of the spaghetti strap, low-cut dress contrasted nicely with her caramel skin and stopped right above her knees, showing off her shapely hips and muscular legs. She had on dark green, strappy heels that brought out the green in the dress. She was absolutely beautiful, probably one of the most beautiful women anyone had ever seen. But she was also extremely deadly.

Queen ran most of the drug operations in the United States and was even the front-runner in some operations abroad. Word was that she had multiple caves that led from the U.S. to Mexico which brought in her large shipments of over ten or more kilos a day. She had a billion dollar operation going and handled everything with an iron fist, just like her father had. Her empire began when she was only sixteen years old, after her father was gunned down at her sweet sixteen birthday party.

Now she was in her early thirties and there was no one who could battle The Queen's Cartel. She let small-time hustlers like Lloyd eat from time to time because they didn't threaten her reign, and it actually worked for her benefit occasionally that she allowed others to have a small come-up, but for the most part, she was that bitch. She was untouchable and unstoppable and, from the looks of it, she was also furious…at Trigga.

Queen stared back at him with a blank expression on her face but didn't say anything right away. Then she turned to her left and it was at that moment that Trigga allowed himself to look at something other than her. In the corner next to where Queen stood with two of her most trusted bodyguards on either side of her, Keisha was in a small chair, strapped down with a rag stuffed in her mouth to stop her from screaming. She was still wearing only the t-shirt that he'd left on her before making love to her; her bottom half was as naked as the day she was born.

"This what you call 'back on it'?" Queen said as she motioned at Keisha who looked horrified. Her eyes were wide and rimmed red. They were also puffy as if she had been crying. "You back on what the fuck I paid you to do or you back on this bitch?"

Trigga flinched when she called Keisha a bitch, but stopped when the big ass bodyguard next to Queen pulled out his gun and pointed it at Keisha's head within seconds.

"Fuck," Trigga said under his breath, too low for them to hear.

This is what annoyed him about caring about someone. They could always be used against you when it came to certain situations. Seeing Keisha sitting across from him with a gun to her head made him heated. But beyond anything, he was frustrated because he knew that although he couldn't do anything in the moment, he was gonna have to put a bullet in the fucker who was holding the gun and that was going to put him at odds with Queen.

"No, what I mean is that I'm trying to figure out what Mase and Lloyd got going on. They are working together. Mase tried to kill me the other day and ended up killing some homeless people. Police pinned their murders on me and I just got out of lock-up," Trigga explained to Queen.

He forced himself not to look back at Keisha because he knew he was seconds away from flipping the fuck out, and it could be tragic since he didn't have a gun. He glanced over at the nightstand that Keisha told him she'd put the Glock he gave her in. It was too far for him to reach for but he'd get to it sooner or later.

"So if that's the case and Mase is the one working with Lloyd, why you fuckin' this bitch who got his name on her ass?" Queen shot out the venomous words like they could cut and they sliced through Trigga like a knife.

His eyes went to Keisha, wide with surprise and then, as if catching himself, he forced his expression to go back to normal. The room was silent except for Queen's laughter.

"Don't tell me you didn't know, Trigga," Queen said as she clicked her tongue with false sympathy. Then she turned to the man who had the gun pointing to Keisha and motioned for him to show Trigga the tattoo. The man grabbed Keisha up roughly and Trigga jumped to his feet. The other guard and Queen both aimed weapons on him but he didn't give a shit.

"You already got one wit' yo' fuckin' name on it, homeboy, so I suggest you stop yo' hands from being so fuckin' reckless," Trigga threatened the man.

The guard shot a look at Queen who had no response. Swallowing hard, he continued his task of raising Keisha to her feet and turning her around, but he did it noticeably gentler than before. When he turned Keisha around, Trigga's eyes locked in on the tattoo that she had right smack-dab in the middle of her right ass cheek: LLOYD with some flowers etched around it.

After Trigga had his eye-fill of the tattoo, he let out a sharp breath of annoyance and focused back on Queen, who was focused on his face with a laugh hidden behind her brown eyes. Trigga could tell she actually thought the entire thing was funny. It still didn't mean any of them were safe. He'd seen Queen shoot someone between the eyes with a smile on her face. He didn't know what happened to her to make her heart so cold; she seemed like she could have been a much softer, gentler, loving woman at one point, but those days were long gone.

"She ain't working wit' Lloyd. You can bet on that shit or I woulda fucked her up my damn self," Trigga told Queen. He shot a look at Keisha who had a guilt-ridden expression on her face. There was a pang in his heart for her but he ignored it and turned back to Queen.

"I got dis shit. Give me a few mo' days and I'll be sending Lloyd's ass to the grave. And that dumbass cousin of his, too," Trigga promised, as he ran his hand over his chin and thought about Lloyd's cousin, Kenyon who he'd seen popping bottles at the club.

"If you were anybody else, I wouldn't hesitate to put a bullet in you, you know that right?" Queen said calmly. "Right now, it looks like you're the one who has betrayed me and Mase is the one actually on the job. When I spoke to him last, he said that Lloyd was dead and you said he wasn't. Now I come here and you fuckin' around on the job."

Queen shot a look at Keisha who still looked as if she wanted to climb under a bridge and die. He could tell she was embarrassed and he was sorry that he'd put her in yet another position of danger.

"But I know you and I know Mase. If anyone is pullin' some shady shit, it's your brother." Queen turned to the man who was holding Keisha. "Let her go," she ordered. Turning back to Trigga, she said, "You have a week to make a move. My brother's dead and the muthafuckas involved are still breathing."

Trigga nodded his head with a frown on his face. Queen was right, he had a job to do and he needed to get back on it. Keisha had his mind fucked up. She wasn't going anywhere, that was definite, but he had to figure out a way to have her and keep his head in the game.

"Last thing," Queen said as she turned to the door and grabbed the handle. "I know Mase is your brother. But if he's up to what I think he's up to, there is nothing that you can do to save him."

If he's up to what I think he's up to, you won't be able to get to him before I do, Trigga thought to himself. He nodded his head at Queen to let her know that he understood. It was the rules of the game.

"Make it quick," Queen told him as she walked out the door. He knew exactly what she meant. Queen understood the type of man Trigga was and she knew there was no way he would let a man walk away with his life after he'd held a gun to his woman.

As soon as the men filed out of the room, Trigga reached over to the other side of the bed and grabbed the pistol out of the top drawer of Keisha's nightstand. Then he jumped up and pulled on his boxers as quickly as possible. Opening the door, Trigga was able to catch them right before they got to the front door. He took aim at the back of the guard's head, the one who had put the gun on Keisha, and pulled the trigger.

Pow!

Queen, who had made sure to be walking on the other side of the man, only stepped to the side when his body fell to her feet. Then she glanced at the other bodyguard who had nearly jumped ten feet in the air at the sound of the gun.

"The fuck you waitin' for?" she asked him with her hands up. Then she pointed at the man's lifeless body. "Pick his ass up and put him in the trunk."

The bodyguard said nothing; he just simply leaned down and, with great effort pulled the man off the carpet. There was a small pool of blood on the tile where his head had lain. When Queen and her man left out the apartment and closed the door, Trigga began to walk towards the blood to clean it up, but he heard a muffled voice coming from behind him. He looked into the room, but it wasn't Keisha; she was kneeling down in the corner with her head on her knees and tears spilling down her face. Trigga wanted to go to her but he had to figure out where the muffled sound was coming from first.

"Tish?" Trigga called out when he opened up her room door.

He looked in and saw that Queen's men had tied Tish down to her bed and put a sock in her mouth as well. Leave it to Queen to make sure she left no stone unturned. Tish was still in her pajamas, a pink lace top and shorts set. She'd probably been sleeping peacefully when they'd grabbed her and tied her to the bed. She was scared senseless and her face was covered with tears. Trigga shook his head and pulled the sock out of mouth then began untying the ropes. Tish let out a loud wail that almost made him want to stuff the sock back down her damn throat but he knew she was traumatized.

"You're okay," was all Trigga said as he walked out of the room. His mind was preoccupied with thoughts of Keisha and her well-being.

"You good?" he asked when he got back into the room. Keisha shook her head from side to side but kept her eyes on the floor.

"I gotta get you out of here. Let's go," Trigga told her. He reached down to grab her arm but she snatched away from him. When she raised her face to look at him, he saw her eyes were filled with tears.

"I'm not going anywhere with you!" she yelled out.

Her words sliced through Trigga's heart like a machete and he stepped back with a deep frown etched into his face.

"Keesh, what the hell you talkin' about?"

"I'm not goin' anywhere with you!" she repeated, standing to her feet. She pushed him as hard as she could and he backed away against the wall, although her strength was nothing to him.

"Ever since I met you my life has been fucked up! You got people I don't even know coming in my house, holding a fuckin' gun to my head, tyin' me up...tyin' Tish up! GET THE FUCK OUT OF HERE TRIGGA AND DON'T COME BACK!" Keisha yelled out.

Trigga's mouth parted slightly as he stared at her. This had been his unspoken worry when it came to Keisha; that she would want to leave when she either found out what it was that he did for a living or if he couldn't get the shit he was in handled quickly.

"Keesh, man, you can't blame me for all this shit! I've been tryin' to protect you from everything. I've been sleepin' outside your fuckin' spot. How the hell you turning this shit on me?" Trigga yelled back at her.

He hated the words that were leaving from his mouth but he couldn't stop himself from saying them. Never before had he begged nan bitch to stay in his life, but this time his heart was talking. How the hell he could feel so strongly about someone who he really knew nothing about, he didn't know. But it was like he knew everything he needed to know. And they'd been through more than the average couple in only a few months. He loved her.

"I can't deal with this shit anymore. I dealt with it with Lloyd. I can't do it," Keisha whined.

Trigga clenched his jaw together as he looked at her. "You can't blame me for the shit that you went through with Lloyd. I ain't that nigga!"

Keisha started crying and he walked over and reached out to her but she backed away. She knew that if she allowed him to touch her, it would all be over and she wouldn't be able to turn him away.

"Trigga, go!" she yelled out and dropped her head in her hands. She was pushed to the furthest point that she could be, still in the corner where Queen's guard had held her. She prayed the Trigga didn't come any closer because if he did, she couldn't fight him any longer.

"Keesh...you been using?" Trigga said suddenly. The sad tone in his voice stopped her from crying instantly.

"What?" Keisha asked him as she sniffed a few times and wiped the tears from her face.

She lifted her head up to see what he was talking about. To her shock and dismay, he was staring at the lines of coke that she'd cut up the day he'd gotten arrested.

"You been using again?" Trigga repeated, this time his voice cracked when he said it.

He turned to face Keisha with his eyes narrowed at her and a disappointed look on his face that crushed her.

"No, I haven't been using!"

"Then what the fuck these lines doing here, Keesh? Where the hell you got this coke from if you've been sober since I saved your ass months ago?"

Trigga walked right in her face and waited for her to respond. Keisha swallowed hard and thought of what she wanted to say. She didn't want to tell him that she'd taken it from Lloyd's condo, along with the money that she'd given Tasha for bailing him out. How could she explain the reason behind taking it unless to admit that she was planning on using it?

"Where is the rest of it?" Trigga asked her solemnly.

Keisha opened her mouth to say something to him but then thought twice about it. There wasn't anything she could say to explain to him why she had the coke. Her intentions had been to use it when she was stressed the fuck out. There was no other excuse.

"It's in the drawer...behind where you pulled the gun from," she said quietly.

Trigga walked over and reached in the drawer, pulling it all the way out. He made a clicking noise with his tongue when he saw the bags of coke and pills, before pulling it out. Each bag that he pulled out made Keisha feel like shit. She had enough drugs in there to send her to prison for life and she didn't know what to tell Trigga.

Maybe I can tell him I was planning to sell it? she asked herself. Then she thought about how she'd just been crying about being held at gunpoint a few minutes ago. Trigga knew she wasn't about that street life.

"Yeah, you right. Me being around has caused more problems for you than help," Trigga said with a blank face.

He looked her in the eyes intensely and then looked away suddenly. It was too hard for him to look at her anymore. The guilt of what him being around was making her do was getting to him. Not only was her life in danger because other people were coming after her, it was in danger because the stress from her situations was driving her to go back to drugs. And from the look of all the product he had in his hands, she was ready to snort and pill-pop herself into a coma.

"I'll leave you money to replace what you paid Tasha. Keep the gun but you won't need to worry about it after a few days."

Trigga dropped the gun on the bed and pulled his shirt over his head. It wasn't until he was buttoning up his pants that he looked at Keisha for what he was certain would be the last time. She was sitting down, wiping tears from her eyes. He gritted his teeth and turned towards the lines on the dresser then opened up one of the bags of coke and dumped the white dust inside before walking out of her bedroom door. It was hard for him to leave but he knew that it was what he had to do.

Sometimes when you love someone, the best thing you can do for them is to let them go.

TWENTY-TWO

"So what's da plan?" Mase asked Lloyd as he blew out a large puff of smoke from the blunt that Lloyd handed him. They were in Lloyd's condo downtown. He told Mase to come over so they could discuss what they were going to do about Queen.

After letting the smoke caress his lungs, Mase stopped, turned the blunt towards his face and stared at it with his face scrunched up.

"Damn, man, what the fuck you got in this shit? This straight weed?"

Lloyd started laughing and nodded his head. "Yeah, nigga, you ain't never had shit better than that, huh?"

Mase nodded his head and took another pull. "It ain't as good as that shit Queen workin' with but it's damn sho' straight!"

Lloyd frowned and batted the blunt out his hand before stomping it into the tile floor.

"Man, what you do dat fah?" Mase whined. He bent down to pick up the smashed up roach off the floor. "I was still smokin' that shit!"

"Then yo' dumb ass opened up your mouth talkin' 'bout how it wasn't better than that shit Queen pushin'. Shoulda kept yo' dumb ass mouth closed, nigga!" Lloyd sat down in his leather armchair and crossed his arms in front of him. On the table in front of him was a pile of weed that he was about to separate into bags. It made up his personal collection.

"Anyways, this is the plan," Lloyd started.

Mase flopped down in the chair across from him with a deep scowl on his face, as he stuffed the beat up blunt in his pocket for later. He was never one to pass up good weed.

"My cousin turned snitch so that nigga gotta go. Soon as I catch up with that rattin' ass nigga, we can use his body for Trigga's and be done wit' that bitch."

And I can be done with you, Lloyd added to himself. It was still his plan to off Mase's stupid ass right after he got the money and product after robbing Queen. Mase was only alive because he was the connection between him and Queen.

"Okay, I got it," Mase said as he nodded his head eagerly. "Where the nigga at?"

"I got my top nigga, AK, stationed outside of the house we found Dior at. Soon as that nigga call me and let me know Kenyon's snitchin' ass back over there, we taking a drive to gut his ass." Lloyd punched his hand into his open palm as he spoke.

Sighing loudly, he shook his head and continued. "I just can't believe that my own blood would pull some shit like that. We were raised like brothers. You never think that yo' blood would betray—"

He stopped short when he remembered who was in his presence and eyed Mase. Mase gave him a blank look which let him know that either he didn't even know where Lloyd was going with that statement or he didn't think he qualified as someone who was doing the same thing Kenyon was doing; betraying his blood.

"Anyways, that's the plan," Lloyd finished and stood up. "Then we done."

"What about the bitch?" Mase asked him as he stood up as well.

"What bitch?" Lloyd furrowed his eyebrows at Mase. "I already killed Dior. That's a done deal. And the baby wasn't mine so I took care of her, too!"

Mase looked like he was about to be sick and staggered from foot to foot a few times. "Man, I ain't about killin' kids…"

"Nigga, you killed yo' own fuckin' twin brother. Shut that shit up!"

Mase dropped his head to the ground and rubbed at the back of his neck. "Man, you ain't have to remind me of that shit. I'm still torn up about that, man. He was a pain in my ass but that nigga ain't deserved to die. Not like that!"

Lloyd walked over and slapped the shit out of Mase, making him stagger backwards a few steps. Mase clutched the side of his face and narrowed his eyes at Lloyd, then barred his teeth.

"Man, what da fuck you hit me fo'?"

"You need to get out yo' fuckin' feelings so we can get this money! This was yo' fuckin' plan and now you over here sobbin' and shit because you killed a nigga you wanted to kill. Get yo' sorry ass up out my spot!" Lloyd yelled at him and pointed towards the door.

Mase shot Lloyd a look and then started walking slowly towards the door. Then it was as if something stopped him mid-step and he swiveled back around. When Lloyd glanced up from the pile of weed that was in front of him, he saw Mase staring at him with an awkward expression on his face.

"What da fuck you want, nigga?" Lloyd sneered at him.

Mase rubbed at the back of his neck and shifted from leg to leg like he had to go take a piss. Lloyd put his hands up in the air as if to signal that Mase better hurry up and get to talking.

"Man, I was just wonderin' if you could front me somethin' until we get the money from Queen," he said in a low tone. Lloyd's eyes nearly bugged out his head.

"Front you some what? I know you ain't askin' me for no money!" he yelled out. He jumped up from his chair and put his hand to his waist to pull out his pistol. He couldn't kill Mase yet but he could pistol-whip his ass to sleep.

Nigga ain't done shit but fuck up and now he wanna ask me for some fuckin' money? For what?

"No! I wouldn't ask you for no money, man!" Mase shouted with his hands in the air, his eyes trained on Lloyd's right hand, which was inching closer and closer to where he kept his gun.

"Well, what da fuck yo' dumb ass askin' me fo' then?" Lloyd gritted.

He crossed his arms in front of his chest and waited for Mase to answer him. But based on Mase's history, he already knew he was about to open up his mouth and let out some stupid shit.

"Some weed!"

Lloyd blinked a few times, unsure that he'd heard him correctly.

Did this nigga just…

"Man, get da fuck out my damn crib! You already fuckin' shit up in yo' regular state of mind!"

Mase looked at him like he couldn't comprehend what he was saying so Lloyd walked over and snapped in front of his face to bring him out of the La La Land he was in.

"Earth to dumb ass! You hear me?" Mase frowned and shot a look at Lloyd before turning to walk towards the door.

"First, I gotta deal with somebody stealing my fuckin' money and shit, now yo' dumb ass—" Lloyd turned back and sat down in his chair. He pulled a bulb and placed it inside of a small baggie.

"Keisha!" Mase yelled out suddenly as a lightbulb went off in his head. "That's the bitch who bit my….she the one who stole yo' shit!"

"Wait….what?!" Lloyd jumped back up out his seat. "She did what?"

"That day that she handled my shit up, if you know what I mean." Lloyd nodded his head quickly not wanting Mase to continue in that direction of conversation. "Anyways, she stole yo' shit and

KEISHA & TRIGGA 2

left. I thought I told you! She cleaned out everything you kept in that room to the side!"

Lloyd paused for a split second only to wonder how the hell Mase knew where he stashed his cash at. He made a mental note to find a new stash spot.

"That bitch gotta go," was all Lloyd said once he was done thinking about what Lloyd had said. He sat back down and started tending to his weed.

"So that's a no to the weed?" Mase asked him again. Lloyd ran his hand over his face and tried to muster up all the patience he could. Fortunately for Mase, that was all he needed and he turned to walk out the door.

"Never had to worry about this shit wit' Trigga," he said under his breath. Lloyd didn't hear all of what Mase said but he did hear the name "Trigga" so he knew it was about some bullshit.

"You know what, how the fuck I even know that nigga dead?" Lloyd asked Mase suddenly.

Mase turned around quickly with a smile on his hideous face. Finally, he was feeling like he'd done something right.

"I took a pic!" He nodded his head like he was the genius in the room and pulled out his cell phone. Lloyd held out his hand for it and Mase walked over to hand it to him.

After pecking at the screen a few times, Lloyd realized he couldn't get in. "What's the damn password, nigga?"

"Password," Mase responded.

"Yes, the password. What is it?" Lloyd shot Mase an annoyed stare.

"Password."

This gate-toothed ass nigga can't be this damn stupid.

"So your password is 'password'?" Lloyd was about two seconds from slapping the monkey shit out of Mase one more time.

"Yeah!" Mase exclaimed as if it was ingenious.

Lloyd shook his head and muttered obscenities under his breath while he unlocked the phone. He flicked through Lloyd's screenshots of naked women and photos that he'd taken of the bullet-hole in his ass then finally settled on something that looked like a body wrapped under covers. The head of the body had a bullet-hole in it and blood was spilling out of the injury.

"NIGGA, WHAT DA FUCK IS THIS?" he yelled out and threw the phone at Mase's head. He ducked and the phone landed on the tile floor, breaking into pieces.

"HEY!" Mase yelled. "What you do that for?"

"How the fuck am I supposed to be able to tell who that is?" Lloyd asked him. He thought about saying fuck him and fuck getting and Queen but knew he couldn't. If he didn't get to Queen first, she would get him and that was reality.

"It's him! I couldn't get—"

Lloyd jumped up and grabbed Mase around his neck. He leaned in close so that Mase was looking him square in the eyes and said to him slowly, through his teeth, "If I find out that you're fuckin' round with me, I will kill you my damn self. That's a muthafuckin' promise."

He released Mase roughly, pushing him hard and making him stumble a few feet away. He had the nagging feeling that he needed to kill Mase right on the spot, but then the next issue would be that he had no inside man to get at Queen. He still needed Mase to deliver a body to her to prove that he was dead. Without that body, she would never stop looking for him. And he was too flashy a nigga to live out his life on the run, hiding from a bitch.

TWENTY-THREE

The sunlight peeked through the bent blinds on Keisha's windows and woke her right up from a good sleep. Tish's nosey ass was the reason that the blinds were in the horrid state they were presently in. Since Keisha's room faced the street and parking lot, Tish was forever coming in and peeking through them so she could see what was going on.

Keisha blinked a few times and then jumped straight up and moved to the blinds. When she looked out, her heart dropped to her stomach. Part of her knew that Trigga wouldn't be out there because he wasn't out there when she fell asleep the night before, but she was still trying to keep hope alive.

So much for that shit, she thought to herself.

"You goin' to class today?" a voice said from the doorway making her jump.

"Tish! Damn! Can't you at least knock or some shit before you walk in my room?" Keisha yelled out.

She walked over to her adjoining bathroom and grabbed her toothbrush. Tish followed behind her.

"I would have but I saw your lonely ass staring out the window like a lost orphan, so I figured I would let you have your moment."

Keisha glared at her as she put toothpaste on her toothbrush but didn't respond. It hadn't even been twenty-four hours and she was already missing Trigga. How could you miss someone who wasn't even part of your life six months ago? She didn't even know anything about Trigga other than the fact that he was mixed up in a lot of shit. A lot of shit that she didn't want anything to do with.

I need to get over him, she thought as she brushed her teeth.

"You're doing the right thing. I've seen women lose their minds and lives over no good niggas. Some bitches don't know when to let go," Tish said sadly as if she were thinking of someone.

Keisha pulled the toothbrush out her mouth and spit into the sink.

"Is that how you got that gash on your face?" she asked her. Tish shook her head and her expression changed to one of anger.

"Naw, a bitch did this but it wasn't about a nigga I was fuckin'." Tish moved her hand to the scar on her cheek. "She was mad because I told her that her baby daddy wasn't shit and had her goin' around the city actin' like a fuckin' fool. Nigga ain't give two shits about her…that's what I mean. Some bitches don't know when to let go."

Keisha nodded and then leaned down to rinse out her mouth without saying anything. She didn't want to mention anything to

Tish but she still hadn't figured out that part yet. She had no idea how she would let go of Trigga.

***

Trigga watched as Kenyon walked out of Grady Hospital and jumped in his cocaine white Mercedes Benz. He used to feel a little excitement when the time to kill was so close, but he felt nothing and he blamed that all on Keisha. He'd only been away from her for about twenty hours, six minutes, forty-five seconds and counting, but he couldn't seem to get her off his mind. So he tried to focus on what he'd promised Queen he would take care of in hopes that it would get his mind off Keisha.

After spending all night looking for information on Lloyd, Mase and Kenyon, he came up with nothing. He spent a whole lot of time searching for bullshit and came up empty handed. Then on a whim, he decided to look up Lloyd's wife's name, Dior Mitchell-Evans, and he finally got a hit. She was in the intensive care unit at Grady Hospital.

After posting up there for a few hours, it wasn't long before he saw Kenyon walking out of the double doors holding a baby. He looked like a homeless man; paranoid as fuck, clothes wrinkled and dirty as hell, and an unkempt beard and hair that was about a week past needing a haircut. It struck Trigga as odd that Kenyon was at the hospital with Lloyd's wife instead of Lloyd, whom he had heard was now out of jail, but he was grateful for the lead anyways.

"This shit is about to be too easy," Trigga said under his breath.

He reached out and grabbed the brand new Glock that he'd purchased off the streets. It was funny how easy it was to get an untraceable weapon in the hood when you had enough dough.

Pulling out of the parking lot of the hospital, Trigga kept his eyes trained on Kenyon's car and followed him out. They cruised through the streets of Atlanta easily then got onto I-75. As Trigga followed behind Kenyon, he couldn't help but think about Keisha. He grabbed his cell phone and fought the urge to dial her number. He always thought niggas who were whipped over a bitch were just pussy. Now here he was doing the same female shit he saw other niggas doing, talking themselves out of making calls.

Trigga laughed at himself as he turned off an exit. A year ago, if a nigga told him that he would be on the job with his mind on a female, he would've laughed in that nigga's face. Now here he was, barely able to focus because his eyes were on Keisha's smooth caramel legs and perky full breasts. He sucked in a breath, and tried to push away the image of her face when she was about to cum, out of his mind. She was so sexy to him whether she meant to be or not.

Trigga came to his senses when he saw Kenyon turn into the parking lot of a small townhome near Lenox mall. It was time to get to work. He parked his whip a few doors down and watched Kenyon, as he jumped out the driver's seat and then went to the back seat to grab the baby out the back. Trigga clicked his tongue and ran his thumb across his bottom lip as he watched. He hadn't thought about the baby. What the hell would he do with it? Drop it off at the hospital?

Not my problem, he thought.

He waited about thirty more minutes for the sun to go down and then he got out of his Porsche and pulled the hood of his black hoodie sweatshirt on his head. The entire block was quiet. It seemed to be an upper-middle class neighborhood and extremely quiet. Just what Trigga needed.

Trigga walked to the back of the townhouse and, just as he suspected, there was a back entrance. He walked along the rest of the house and peeked in the windows to see if Kenyon was downstairs. He was nowhere to be found so Trigga assumed that he was upstairs. Probably putting the kid to sleep or something.

Walking back to the back of the townhouse, Trigga pulled out a small pick and pushed into the handle of the door. After twisting it a few times, Trigga felt the pressure release and knew the door was now open. He put the pick back in his pocket and felt for his gun before slowly opening the door.

The townhouse was completely empty, except for a few boxes. Either Kenyon had just moved in or he was getting ready to leave. He knew that this wasn't the place where Dior was shot because her hospital records referenced an address in Norcross, that he wanted to check later to see if Lloyd was living there.

Trigga closed the door behind him and crept up the stairs slowly. He could hear some humming from upstairs which told him that that's where Kenyon was with the baby he'd been holding. Trigga pulled out his gun and bent down low as he neared the only lit room down the hall. Peeking around the corner, he expected to see

Kenyon standing over the bassinet in front of him but there was nothing.

Crinkling his eyebrows into a frown, Trigga stopped in his tracks when he heard movement behind him. Swirling around, he lifted his gun up and realized that he was a second too late; Kenyon already had his gun drawn and focused on him.

But what Kenyon didn't understand was that Trigga wasn't your average dude. A regular dude would have frozen at the sight of a nigga pointing a gun at him. But that wasn't Trigga. No matter what gun was pointed at him, if he was able to take a shot, he took it. That's why they called him Trigga.

Pow!

"AHHHHHH, SHIT!" Kenyon yelled out and dropped to his knees.

The shot in his side was already dripping blood. Trigga made sure to put a bullet right below his chest, on the side where he had the gun raised because he knew the shot would make him drop the gun as a reflex. And it did just that. Kenyon released the gun from his hand and it fell to the floor then ricocheted across the room.

"Where the fuck is Lloyd?" Trigga inquired as Kenyon held his side.

"I don't fuckin' know but you better hope you get to that nigga before I do because I'mma murk his muthafuckin' ass," Kenyon sneered through his teeth, as he doubled over in pain and tried to press hard against the womb on his side.

His remark caught Trigga off guard. Why the hell did Lloyd's cousin want him dead? Kenyon must have sensed Trigga's confusion because he noted his expression, chuckled a little and then went on to explain.

"Nigga put my bitch in the hospital and his own fuckin' baby in the oven. I can't wait to kill his ass."

"Damn," was all Trigga could say.

This shit was getting crazier by the second. Now he was finding out that Dior and Kenyon were together and Lloyd had apparently tried to kill her and the baby. What the fuck would make a nigga want to kill his own child? On top of that, him and Kenyon had a common enemy.

"Man, I ain't got no beef wit' you," Kenyon told him. "My issue is wit' Lloyd and that's it. I been working wit' the police to get that nigga locked up and now he tryin' to kill me. I just gotta get him 'fore he get me."

Trigga nodded his head and thought about the baby that Kenyon had stashed somewhere in the house, because she damn sure wasn't in the bassinet. He didn't quite trust him but didn't want to be responsible for creating an orphan. He knew firsthand what it was like growing up in the foster care system. After his mother died, he was left at the mercy of the state and one thing he learned was the state had no mercy.

"A'ight," Trigga said. He turned away and prepared to leave. His phone buzzed in his pocket and his first thought was that it was Keisha although he knew it wasn't her.

Kenyon eyed the gun on the floor as soon as Trigga walked away. His heart had been beating the fuck out of his chest, when he saw Trigga jump out of the Porsche truck that was parked down the way from the house, and it still hadn't stopped. The fact that Lloyd was out and his goons had gotten to Dior and Karisma had him in a state of paranoia that he'd never experienced before. He'd always been a thug but he'd always had a team of thugs on his side, also. Now he was seeing that this shit wasn't so easy when you were rocking by yourself.

As soon as Trigga rounded the corner, Kenyon bent down and grabbed the gun off the ground. He believed that Trigga was a man of his word and he knew that he could have killed him, but one thing that Kenyon had learned was that you never point a gun at a nigga and don't shoot his ass dead. That shit would come back around to bite you in the ass every time. So the bottom line was, Trigga had to die.

With the gun in his hand, Kenyon shot down the hallway, careful to keep his footsteps light. When he bent around the corner, he ran smack into a cold piece of steel.

"A snitch can never be trusted," Trigga said with an icy tone. *Pow!*

TWENTY-FOUR

When her professor dismissed the class, Keisha bolted out of the room so fast that she almost walked straight out of her red hot Balenciaga sandals. And it wasn't even because of the fact that Tasha had been sitting in the back corner staring holes into the side of her face either. She couldn't focus and every second she found herself glancing over her shoulder.

Every dark-skinned man in the classroom looked like Lloyd to her. When she walked around campus, she just knew that people thought she was crazy. Her eyes were wide and she surveyed every single face as she walked carefully trying to make sure that she wasn't being watched. The very thing that she was doing to not be noticed made her the most noticeable person in the area, but she couldn't get herself to relax. She had late classes this evening so it was dark when she walked outside and everyone moving around her made her jump because she couldn't see all that clearly.

I'm buggin' like a muthafucka, Keisha thought to herself.

Exhaling sharply, Keisha walked to the water fountain to get a drink and try to calm herself down. She couldn't take another hour of this. She was going to have to catch the bus back home and skip her next class. It was getting darker by the minute and she just wanted to get home before nightfall. At the rate that she was going, she'd be withdrawing before she even reached the mid-term exams. Her dreams of finishing her degree and leading a normal life were quickly fading away.

"Hey, you alright?" a voice said from behind her.

Although the voice sounded friendly, Keisha still damn near jumped twenty feet in the air before she turned around to the source of the greeting while clutching onto her chest. She tried to relax when her eyes fell upon a familiar face, a cute guy from her class with the build of a football player. Keisha was almost positive that he did in fact play sports from the way she'd seen some of the other younger girls swooning over him in class.

He was tall, muscular and had the prettiest big brown eyes that anyone had ever seen on a man. He had smooth chocolate skin and kinda reminded her of Morris Chestnut in his younger days but he had Drake's preppy boy, gangster swag. He was the type of guy who came into class always looking fly but you never knew who you were going to get: the sexy ass nerdy boy, the jock, or the intelligent looking thug. He had a versatile style and it was attractive, but Keisha had instantly dismissed him as being too young for her. Since she'd waited to get back into college, she was a couple years older than the other students in her classes.

"I'm good. Thanks," Keisha told him with a slight nod of her head. She didn't offer him a smile or anything. She didn't want to give him a reason to start a conversation with her.

"I'm Chris. We had that last class together. You looked like something was bothering you."

Keisha continued to walk to the bus stop without giving him an answer. She hoped that not saying anything was the answer he needed to make him keep moving.

"You gone ignore me like that, ma?" he asked in a smooth, teasing way.

Keisha could hear the smile in his voice. Rolling her eyes, she turned back to him. Just as she suspected, he was standing there with a smirk on his face.

"Oh, you're used to women havin' your full, undivided attention, huh?" she shot back at him and placed her hand on her hip. She could tell that she caught him off guard because the smirk fell from his face as he processed what she was saying, and then he suddenly started to laugh.

"Am I bein' judged off what you seen other females do? All attention ain't wanted."

Keisha took a deep breath and then turned around just in time to see her bus pull up to the stop. She took off in a jog to the bus and got there just in time. The older, black woman who was driving the bus had an annoyed expression all over her face, like she'd worked a full day and didn't want to make it last a second longer.

Keisha shot her an apologetic glance before finding her seat. When she sat down, she was surprised to see that Chris was right behind her. She rolled her eyes again and let out a loud sigh when he sat down in the seat right next to her.

"This is not your bus," Keisha said to him. She knew for a fact that he had a car. It was a blood-red Corvette, something that she'd expect a spoiled, attractive jock to drive.

"It is now," Chris beamed at her, showing off a deep dimple in his left cheek. The dim lighting on the bus, shined on his face at the perfect angle to highlight his handsome features.

Keisha found herself smiling back at him before she knew it. She shook her head and looked out the window, which was her last attempt at trying to ignore Chris. It was getting pretty hard to do it; his persistence was actually flattering her. It was a sharp difference from how Trigga had been when she met him. He seemed so uninterested in her although she felt he was attracted to her. It was a strange encounter but he still pulled her in.

I have to stop thinking about him, she thought to herself as she looked out the window.

"You live near here?" Chris' voice interrupted her thoughts but she was grateful for it. Maybe conversation was what she needed to stop thinking about the man she couldn't have.

"Yeah, about a couple blocks."

"Okay, well here." Chris pushed his iPhone into her hand. Keisha grabbed on to it and frowned at him.

"What's this for?"

"If you live close, I don't have time for all the back and forth shit. Just put your number in there so I can give you a call when I come to take you out," Chris said as if it was a sure thing and there was nothing to talk over with Keisha.

Shaking her head, Keisha was about to push the phone right back at Chris and decline but then she stopped. Chris seemed like the good guy; smart, college student, possibly an athlete. He dressed nice, had clean teeth and didn't strike her as a thug. Sure, he seemed like he was boring as hell but maybe boring was what she needed. Maybe she'd be fine if she wasn't awakened in the middle of the night by a woman who had a gun to her temple.

"Okaaaaayyyy," Keisha agreed slowly. She keyed her number in quickly and handed the phone back to Chris. He pressed a button and a few seconds later Keisha's phone was ringing.

"Now you have my number," he said to her. They locked eyes for a minute and then finally Keisha nodded.

"This is my stop," she said to him when she noticed the bus had come to a halt right in front of her apartment. She stood up and waited for Chris to allow her to pass through.

"I'll walk you off."

Keisha didn't respond. She walked to the front of the bus and looked up when she felt eyes on her face. It was the driver and she had a slick ass grin on her face.

"Pretty ass boy wore you down, huh?" she said with a toothy grin like watching the two of them had made her day.

Keisha tried to hide her embarrassment and turned to walk out the doors of the bus. As soon as they opened, she found herself looking right into Trigga's light brown eyes. He was frowning as he stood in front of the bus wearing a black hoodie, black sweatpants and some black expensive looking sneakers. Keisha's mouth parted slightly and she stopped right in her tracks as she looked into his eyes.

"Bye, Keisha," Chris said from behind her. He touched her lightly on the arm and she turned around to look at him. "I'll give you a call later on tonight."

"No the fuck you won't," Trigga answered for her with his eyes narrowed in on Chris. Keisha gasped and brought her hands to her face which was flushed red with the shame she felt.

"Trigga!"

"Aw, shit! She done got caught up!" the driver said from behind Keisha's back. A long day at work had turned into the best scene of Maury right before her eyes.

"Look man, I ain't meant no harm," Chris responded with his hands in the air. Keisha turned around sharply and gawked at him. He was so persistent with her but here he was giving in to Trigga on the first opportunity!

This why the fuck I only mess with thugs...

"Keesh, get your ass down here!"

With a frown and her face cherry-red from embarrassment, Keisha sucked her teeth and walked off the bus, glaring at Trigga the entire way. When she got off, she stood right in front of him and, although she was trying to keep her attitude, she was losing it fast. He was standing over her and frowning down at her so deeply, but it was sexy at the same time. She couldn't tell whether she should yell at him for shaming her in front of all the people on the bus or if she should jump in his arms, wrap her legs around him and beg him to undress her.

"Who the fuck was that clown ass nigga on the damn bus all up in yo' fuckin' face?" Trigga asked as his eyes bore down into hers.

Keisha noticed that the bus still hadn't pulled off so she turned around slowly and shot the driver a look. The woman grunted and finally moved to close the doors and continued on her way. Keisha let her eyes fall to the seat that Chris was in, but he was looking straight ahead as if he hadn't just heard what Trigga said about him.

"I know you heard what the fuck I—"

"I heard you, Trigga! Damn!" Keisha said with frustration. She glanced around the parking lot to see if anyone else was within earshot of their conversation before answering.

"He's someone from my class!"

"So what the hell he doin' all up in yo' damn face on the bus? Don't look like y'all were discussing formulas and shit to me. What was that you put up in that nigga phone? I know it wasn't no fuckin' Pentagon Theorem!"

Keisha had to bite her lip to keep herself from laughing at the way Trigga was going off. It was cute and sexy.

"You mean the Pythagorean Theorem, Trigga?" Keisha teased him with a smile. She punched him in his side playfully.

"Man, don't fuckin' correct me. What the hell you gave that nigga?" he repeated.

Trigga wasn't backing down any time soon. He was mad as hell. The entire time he'd been away from Keisha all he did was think about was her. He couldn't get her off his mind so, even though he knew he was dead ass wrong, he took a break after dealing with Kenyon and getting a good night's rest, then hopped in the whip and went straight to wait for Keisha to get home.

Then after replaying a bunch of warm and fuzzy love shit in his mind of how it would be when he first saw her, he sees her bus pull up with some lame ass, college nigga grinning all up in her face. And to prove that he was the punk that Trigga thought he was, as soon as he was called out, he retreated. His punk ass wasn't even worthy of the phone number Trigga knew she'd given him.

"Trigga, let's go in the house, pleeeeaaaase," Keisha begged. "I missed you."

Trigga's attitude fell a little when she wrapped her arms around him and kissed him softly on his cheek. He bent down and pressed his lips against her soft lips.

"I missed you too, Keesh."

"Well, come inside and show me how much," she teased. A goofy grin crossed Trigga's face and he held on to her hand as she led him to the front door. But when she opened the door and tried to tug him inside, he was reminded of one of the reasons that he had come over in the first place.

"Oh, shit! The baby!"

"Baby?" Keisha nearly yelled.

Trigga released her hand and she whipped around to see what was going on. She watched as he opened up the back door of his car, this time a black Benz SUV, and pulled out a small baby. Keisha threw her hands on her hips and got ready for the attitude that she was about to have. She knew damn well Trigga wasn't bringing a baby of his up in her spot. And the baby looked brand new, too!

"Trigga, you need to take that baby back to your baby mama and your ass can stay over there with it. Who the fuck do you think I am? That's a brand new fuckin' baby—"

"Man, Keesh, chill! Damn! This ain't my baby. It's Lloyd's," Trigga revealed to her.

Keisha gasped and covered her mouth with her hands as she moved to the side to let him in. After peeking around outside the door, she closed it and turned to Trigga.

"What you mean that's Lloyd's baby! Why is it…why is she here?"

Trigga bit the inside of his cheek. He told himself on the way over that he was going to talk with Keisha and let her know what he did, but now he was thinking that it was probably better to go with a lie. But there was no lie on Earth that could make sense of the reason why he was holding Lloyd and Dior's baby.

Trigga exhaled, pushed the baby into Keisha's arms and then sat down on the couch behind him. Keisha held the baby awkwardly at first as she frowned down at her. But then the baby cooed and she seemed to relax a little.

"Sit down, I need to talk to you," Trigga said suddenly.

The intensity of his words made Keisha nervous. She sat down immediately right in front of him, cupping the small baby in her arms. Trigga took a long, deep breath and then started to fill her in on everything from the beginning.

TWENTY-FIVE

It wasn't until Trigga touched her lightly on her leg that Keisha snapped out of the trance that she was in. She felt like she was sitting in a parallel universe and wasn't sure what was real and what was fake. She looked down into her arms when she felt the baby squirming.

"What are we supposed to do with her?" Keisha asked finally.

It was the only thought that she could focus on at the moment. Trigga had just told her that he was a hired killer and he and Mase had been sent to Atlanta to kill Lloyd. It made her think back to the moment that she'd been furious and held a gun in her own hand, aimed it at Dior's belly with full intention to shoot. In her drug-induced rage, she would have killed the child that she was now holding in her arms. She held the baby tightly to her chest as if silently begging for the little girl to forgive her. She seemed to coo in her arms and it made Keisha smile.

"Well, first we gotta feed it," Trigga shrugged and then eyed the child as Keisha held her tightly.

"She's a girl, Trigga," Keisha rolled her eyes and kissed the child on the forehead. She didn't even know it but she'd been born into a load of bullshit and still managed to look like the happiest child Keisha had ever seen.

"Okay, well, we gotta feed *her* and then we need to drop her ass off at the hospital where her mother is. Only reason I ain't do it right after I left from over there was because when I drove up there, the five-o was out heavy. So I decided to stop by and see how you were doin'. Then you pull up on the bus cheesin' at that whack-ass nigga!"

Keisha lifted her head to frown at him briefly and then turned back to the baby. Trigga felt like he was seeing a premonition as he stared at Keisha while she held the baby in her arms. She looked so motherly in that instant and for a split second, it made him wonder what it would be like to settle down one day and have a child. Shaking his head suddenly, he pushed that thought from his mind almost as soon as it came. There was no need to entertain a thought like that because at this point in his life it was damn near impossible.

"Ay Keesh, I kno' that I just told you a lot of shit and it will take some time adjusting to it, but just let me take care of Lloyd and make sure you're safe. Then you can go on your way wit' that corny ass nigga and I'll go on mine," Trigga joked quietly to try and lighten the effect of his statement. He tried to avoid looking at Keisha directly, so he wouldn't start back having delusions about the family life he could never have.

"Let's not talk about all that right now," Keisha told him. She ran her finger softly down the bridge of the baby's nose repeatedly and watched as the little girl's eyes grew heavy.

"What the hell you doin'?" Trigga asked her with his nose crinkled up.

"Helping her to get sleepy. You ain't never heard of this?"

"Do I look like a babysittin' ass nigga?" Trigga sat back and crossed his arms in front of his face, donning a full frown.

Keisha scoffed and twisted up her lips at him before sucking her teeth. When it all was said and done, if Trigga was serious about leaving, she knew she would miss his rude ass. She kissed the baby on the forehead and whispered, to herself, a thanks to God for stopping her from shooting Dior and then stood up and looked at Trigga. He had an odd look on his face and she couldn't place what he was thinking. Then, as if catching himself, his expression went back to neutral and he stood up too.

"Alright, so we can do the ditch and drive?" Trigga asked with all seriousness in his tone.

"Don't say it like that! You make it seem like we gone chuck the baby out the window and drive away!"

"What? Hell, that's what da fuck we doin'! Leaving her ass at the hospital and dipping!" Trigga argued back. He opened the front door for Keisha to walk out and waited for her to walk through. When he noticed she wasn't moving, he turned back around.

"The fuck you lookin' at me like that for?" Trigga shot back at her. Then a smirk flashed across his face and Keisha had to bite her lip from returning his smile.

"You so muthafuckin' ignorant!" Keisha said shaking her head.

Trigga flicked his tongue out at her like he was a small child then waited for walk by him before he swatted her on the ass. She turned around and glared at him.

"Don't act like a nigga ain't been all up and through that, gul," Trigga teased her, as he locked her door from the inside and closed it behind him.

Damn, I'mma miss her sexy ass.

TWENTY-SIX

With great effort, finally Dior slowly opened her eyes. When she peered through the tiny slits of her eyelids, all she saw was a blaring white light. She squeezed her eyes back closed and tried to avoid the panic that was rising up in her body.

Oh my God! Am I dead?

The feeling of her heart beating in her chest like a sledgehammer was the only thing that clued her into the fact that she was most likely not dead. Taking a deep breath, Dior tried once more to open her eyes, this time slower than before. When she finally came to, this time she found her staring into the dark blue eyes of a heavy-set white man wearing a nice designer suit and sporting a wide-brim fedora. Kind of old fashioned, but it worked for him anyways.

"Mrs. Evans? I'm Detective West," the man said. He was hovering right over her and when he spoke, his stale breath rolled off his tongue and went straight up her nostrils. Dior wrinkled her nose and held her breath for about five beats.

"I'm Dior. Who are you?" she asked. Her voice cracked a little as she spoke. She looked around the room. "Am I in the hospital?"

The man shot her a gloomy look and then nodded his head slowly. Dior blinked a few times and then, like a flash of lightning, her memories suddenly flashed in her mind. When she finally was able to focus on the face of the man in front of her, she had tears running down her cheeks.

"My daughter…is my daughter, okay?" she sobbed.

The man looked uncomfortable and his eyes drifted off to the side. Dior knew then to expect the worst. "Well, we… we were told that the paramedics saw Kenyon cradling a small child when they retrieved you."

"Oh, thank God," Dior breathed out, closing her eyes. "My baby is alive."

Although Karisma wasn't right in front of her face, which is what she would have preferred, she was grateful to hear that her daughter hadn't been killed by her own father. She turned back to the Detective.

"Well, where is Kenyon? Is he here?" she asked with her eyes darting around the room. "And I don't feel any pain at all…am I on pain medication?"

The man shot her another look that made her feel uncomfortable because she couldn't read it at all.

"Mrs. Evans—"

"Dior," she corrected.

"Dior…I need to tell you a few things that may be a little hard to hear. Kenyon…Mr. St. Michaels was found murdered at a townhouse in Buckhead. From the looks of it and knowing what I know about this case, I'm thinking that your husband may have had something to do with it. There was no baby in the house so we think Lloyd may have the child. We've been waiting for three days for you to wake up so we could ask you some…"

Detective West continued speaking but Dior couldn't hear anything he was saying. The only thing that kept ringing in her head was that Kenyon was dead and Lloyd had her baby. She felt the entire room closing in on her and she began to breath heavily like a panic attack was slowly coming in. She felt it but she couldn't stop it. Every second that she thought about her daughter being with Lloyd and Kenyon being dead, intensified the feeling of dread that washed over her entire body.

Looking up suddenly with her eyes filled with tears, Dior tried to reach out and grab the Detective to make him stop talking, but her arms were pinned down to her side. Confused, she looked down to see what was holding her in place, afraid that it might have been handcuffs. But there was nothing. She tried once again to move her limbs and her breathing quickened when she realized that she couldn't. She looked up with desperation etched all over her face, her eyes begging Detective West for an explanation.

"I—I'm going to get your doctor in here so he can speak to you. One second," Detective West muttered and ran out of the room.

Seconds later, a pale white man in a white coat with a baldhead, which only had a few strands of placid silver gray hairs on top walked in wearing large glasses propped up on his thin nose. His lips were in a straight line and he held a folder in his hand as he approached her. He looked at the monitor near her bed before turning to her with a blank expression on his face.

"I'm Doctor Stephens. How are you feeling, Mrs. Evans?" he asked her. Dior just stared back at him with tears falling down her face and her bottom lip quivering from the grief that she felt. She didn't even try to correct him.

"Okay, um…" Doctor Stephens started. His eyes shifted to the side and then he exhaled. "Mrs. Evans, you are paralyzed from the neck down for the most part. You may have a little sensation left that may feel like you can feel your limbs, however, you're unable to move them. Sometimes this state is temporary, sometimes it's permanent. In times like these, the only thing we can do is wait and hope for the best. Now, there are many options for—"

The doctor couldn't get another word out before Dior opened up her mouth and let out a bloodcurdling scream that could be heard down the hall of the busy hospital. They probably heard her in the entire wing. Doctor Stephens jumped backwards in surprise at her wail, but Dior wasn't concerned for him at all. The anguish that she felt for losing the man she loved along with her child was more than she could bear. But to add that, the fact that she'd lost the use of her limbs and would forever be at the mercy of someone else only added to the misery she felt.

In that moment, she wished that Lloyd had succeeded with what he had set out to do. She wished that he'd killed her, too.

TWENTY-SEVEN

It had been three days since Keisha had seen Trigga and the only thing that helped to keep her mind off him was to stay busy. But now she was at the point where she had absolutely nothing to do. Her apartment was clean, dinner was ready, she was caught up on all of her lectures and she had even organized her closet. There literally was nothing else that she could think of to do, so she was sitting on her bed taking off the toenail polish that she had just put on the day before, in order to keep her mind from wandering.

At least five times that day she found herself scrolling to his name in her phone but punking out before she would make the call. Although they hadn't known each other that long, there was so much about her every day that reminded her of him. When she made coffee, she thought of the day she made breakfast for him and took it out to his car. When she went to class, she was reminded of him every time she saw Chris; who, by the way, had been avoiding locking eyes with her. The one time they did happen to glance at each other at the same time, he ducked his head and looked away.

LEO SULLIVAN & PORSCHA STERLING

Keisha laughed to herself, thinking about how he was a punk ass nigga, just like Trigga said he was.

When she went to bed at night, she dreamed of the time she'd gone to sleep wrapped up in his arms. He was the perfect lover; soft but rough at the same time. It was just like his personality. The perfect mix of thug and gentleman. He was everything she needed and wanted. He was even a little of what she didn't know she needed. He was protective of her even when he barely knew her. She'd known Lloyd for years and he turned her into his junkie and didn't think anything of it. He didn't care that she was blowing her life away. He didn't love her and that's why he made her his side bitch.

Trigga was different in every way.

"You goin' to class tomorrow?" Tish's voice erupted through Keisha's thoughts, making her jump and mess up the polish on her big toe.

"Damn, you need to announce your presence. Nobody can hear you creepin' up wit' them light ass steps!" Keisha fumed.

Tish laughed but it didn't seem genuine, almost forced. Keisha was scared to ask what was wrong because she knew she would feel guilty if Tish was still affected by what happened days ago with Queen. But when she looked at the sad expression in Tish's face, she knew that she had to say something to her.

"You okay?"

Tish shook her head. She could see that there was something wrong with her because it looked like she was choking back tears.

Her mouth was curled down at the edges and her eyes danced around various spots on the floor. Keisha dropped the bottle of nail polish and walked over to Tish.

"What is it?"

"Luxe…I think Luxe is cheating on me," Tish said to her. The tears she'd been holding in fell and she swiped them away with the back of her hand. "I really shouldn't care all that much. I mean, we only been messing around for a few months but—"

"But you thought it was something real," Keisha finished, reflecting back on how she felt when she saw Trigga walking out with Tasha at the jail that one day. She knew exactly how her girl felt.

"Yeah," Tish said quietly. "But it's a'ight, I should've know not to mess with a bitch like her anyways. She's used to being pulled by the highest bidder."

"You know who it was she cheated with? Was it someone from the club?" Keisha asked. She back down on the bed and beckoned for Tish to sit down beside her. It seemed a little selfish to admit it, but listening to Tish's problems did temporarily distract her from her own.

"I don't know who it was. All I know is I called her and she must have accidentally hit the button to answer when she thought she had hung up. I said 'hello' and the next sound I heard was her slurping up some dick. There was some nigga in the background callin' her a nasty bitch. I thought maybe she was at the club and she had left her phone somewhere…I was hoping it was some other nasty ass bitch I was hearing, but then I heard Luxe's voice and I knew it was her." Tish sniffed and wiped away more tears before she exhaled heavily and cleared her throat.

"It's all good though. Can't turn a hoe into a housewife…or husband. Hell, it was my first time doin' that shit. I don't know who was the man and who was the woman. Either way, I'm done with women and their emotional asses. I'm back strictly dickly."

Keisha snorted out a small chuckle and then rubbed Tish on her back. "Don't let one cheatin' bitch make you bitter. Niggas ain't shit either."

Tish wiped the last of her tears from her eyes and then lay back on Keisha's bed. She pulled a pillow under her head and exhaled one more time.

"So, I guess that means you and Trigga are done for good? I've seen the way you been moping around the damn house with your jaw draggin' the floor."

Now it was Keisha's turn to exhale heavily. She grabbed her phone and thumbed through until she got to his number. Then she shook her head and clicked on the button to look at their text messages. She frowned when she saw the last text that Trigga had sent her. It wasn't lit up like a new message but it was her first time seeing it.

There's always love for you here, Keesh…with your confused ass.

Likewise, Keisha responded quickly and then dropped the phone beside her. She tried to hold in a laugh as she thought back to the last time she saw him.

They had just dropped off the baby. Trigga didn't want either of them going anywhere near where there would be cameras, so instead of going to the hospital, which had cameras in the parking lot, they drove to the fire station across the street, left her by the door and drove away. Trigga circled the building and saw that a few of the firemen were on an outside area playing cards and laughing, so they went back to the front and he threw a big ass boulder at the door and muttered 'Get y'all asses up'.

When they drove back around, the game was on pause and some of the men had run back inside to investigate the source of the noise. Keisha started laughing as Trigga whipped through the traffic.

Back at her apartment, the mood changed instantly. There was a sadness in the air but neither one of them spoke right away. They were both waiting for the other to say something. Finally, right when Keisha was just about ready to climb in his lap and pretend that everything she knew about him wasn't the truth, Trigga cleared his throat and prepared to speak.

"My deadline is approaching so I gotta get the job done. Then I'll be back in New York..."

He stopped speaking but Keisha waited for him to continue. It didn't seem like he had finished his statement. When she turned to look in his eyes, she saw that they seemed clouded over, like he was struggling with something he needed to say.

"You sure you don't want to come with me?" he asked her with a frown on his face. His words came out strange, almost as if he was forcing himself not to say them.

He was struggling because he didn't want to ask. It felt like he was begging her for some shit that, if she really felt like she said she felt about him, he wouldn't need to ask her about in the first place.

Keisha paused and looked out the window and felt tears coming to her eyes.

"I don't know what to do. It's like if I stay, it's a problem. If I go, it's a problem. When does all this end?"

Trigga frowned at the side of her head as she looked out the window. Then he slammed the car in 'park' and leaned back in his seat. Keisha snapped her neck around to look at him.

"Man, what da fuck does that backwards ass shit mean, Keesh?"

Keisha threw her hands in the air and gave Trigga a look as if to ask if there was a reason he couldn't understand English.

"It MEANS that I don't know where this could even go! How can we have a family? What if I want to have babies? With the kind of work you do, how is a normal life even possible?"

Trigga didn't want to admit it, but she had struck a nerve when she mentioned that because it was something he'd thought about, too. Especially when she was holding Lloyd's baby in her arms. But he didn't have an answer for it, and he was angry at himself for even thinking that he wanted something that he wasn't sure he could have, so it pissed him off even more that she'd mentioned it.

"Ay, just get the fuck out the car with your confused ass!" Trigga said suddenly.

Keisha's eyes widened and she just gawked at him for a few seconds. She couldn't believe how rude he was acting. Then her facial expression softened when she realized that this was his version of pouting. Trigga was the type of man who didn't know how to deal with his emotions; he had no idea how to even communicate his feelings because they were emotions that he wasn't used to feeling. So instead, he fell back on his anger when he got frustrated with himself.

"I love you, too, Trigga," Keisha said after looking at the side of his face for a while.

She waited for him to respond but he didn't move. He continued to stare straight ahead with his wrinkled brow, hovering over his light-colored eyes and his bottom lip damn near in a full pout. He looked like an angry three-year-old; only thing he was missing was the crossed arms in front of his chest. Then, as soon as she thought it, he huffed out a sigh and crossed his arms in front of his chest. It was at that moment that she knew she loved him and if he ever asked her again, she would leave with him.

"If I go with you to New York, would you stop doing what you do?" she asked him softly. She couldn't see her living a full life *the way that she'd lived the last couple months. She needed him to assure her that she could be happy, secure and safe without looking over her shoulder every few minutes for someone to jump out and kill her.*

"It's like if a nigga work, it's a problem. If he don't work, it's a problem. Where does it allllll end?" Trigga mocked her.

Keisha glared at him and grabbed the handle of her door. "Your ass is RUDE!" she barked at him and jumped out of his car.

"And your ass is CONFUSED!" he said just as she slammed the door closed.

As soon as the door closed, Trigga threw the Porsche in reverse and sped out the parking lot. Keisha sat in front of her apartment watching him with her hands on her hips and a scowl on her face. She had no idea that he'd deliberately made himself pick a fight with her so that he didn't have to tell her 'goodbye'. It was the only way he knew he'd be able to leave.

"Helllooooo...Bish, is you sleep?" Tish snapped in front of Keisha's face a few times, jarring her from her thoughts and bringing her back into the room. Keisha jumped back on the bed and shot her a look.

"Damn, Tish! Does it look like my eyes are closed?"

"Might as well be, hell, you ain't talkin'! Lookin' off into space and some shit. Lemme guess, thinkin' about that mafia affiliated nigga, huh?" she flipped her hair back and then placed her hand on her hip before rolling her eyes at Keisha.

Keisha gave Tish a blank look and then burst out laughing. "The mafia?"

"He is in some gang or something but what I do know is it ain't small-time. That bitch that was walkin' around here with them big ass steak-eatin', body-building muthafuckas who tied me up looked like she could shatter bricks with her damn eyeballs. When I woke up and the one with the waves in his head was tying me up while the other one watched, I thought I was about to live out a damn 'thug-love' fantasy of mine until she waltzed her ass up in the room with her evil self!"

Tish frowned and crossed her arms in front of her large breasts that were about an inch away from spilling out of her low-cut halter-top. She looked sincerely upset about the fact that Queen's men were coming on some goon shit rather than to help her live out her fantasy.

"Girl, you stupid!" She fell out laughing on the bed.

Three hours later, they had laughed and joked about their relationships and battles with love over pizza and were drunk as hell after mixing all the leftover liquor they had in their makeshift bar and making the strongest drinks they could concoct. Keisha yawned loudly and shook her head, before she fell back on her pillows and rubbed her eyes. Tish had been mid-sentence, ranting about how much of a freak that Luxe had been and how it should have told her 'that hoe wasn't loyal', when she fell right to sleep.

Keisha reached out to her nightstand and grabbed her remote to turn off the stereo on her dresser that was crooning the latest album from The Weekend. It was Keisha's new favorite. With the music off, the only thing that could be heard was Tish's soft snores. Keisha nudged her a bit on the side with her elbow, making her shift in her sleep to her side, and the snoring came to halt. Finally, able to enjoy some peace and quiet, she drifted off to sleep.

But when she closed her eyes, all she could see was Trigga's face.

TWENTY-EIGHT

"When you gone take me somewhere? I wanna go out to eat or somethin'. You just want to fuck all day?" Luxe asked and whipped her hair to the side as she sucked her teeth.

She tried to run her hand through her hair but was stopped when her fingers came into contact with matted up hair.

"Ewww, this shit is nasty! You gone give me some money to get my hair done?" she asked him with her lips twisted up.

"Bitch, you need to come over here and do what da fuck I paid you to do first. All that fuckin' mouth. Why don't you close your mouth around this damn dick!" Lloyd snapped.

He pushed the silk covers off of his naked body and reached out to grab his blunt and lighter. Lighting the end, he pulled hard on the blunt, laid his head back on his leather-upholstered headboard and waited for Luxe to pull his limp dick into her mouth. Two seconds passed and he didn't feel her soft, silky lips around his pole so he lifted his head up sharply to see what the holdup was.

"Bitch! Yo' Mexican ass don't understand my damn English?"

Luxe scowled at him and then sucked her teeth again as she crawled over to him slowly. Lloyd focused in on her big, bouncy titties as they swayed from side to side while she crawled. His nature began to rise immediately.

"A'ight, papi, but I ain't Mexicano. Soy Cubano," she corrected him in Spanish.

"'Soy' betta start suckin' on this muthafuckin' dick-o before 'Soy' find a bullet-o in yo' damn ass-o!" Lloyd chided.

Luxe rolled her eyes at him and just as Lloyd was about to click on her and smack her cross the room, she lowered her head and used her mouth like a vacuum, suctioning his pole into her mouth like a pro.

"Gotdaaaaammmmmn," Lloyd moaned. He tilted his head back on the headboard and placed the blunt back between his lips, as he enjoyed the service she was providing.

Luxe was the perfect remedy for the frustration he was feeling because of the bullshit that he found himself in. His way of dealing was to call up Luxe, a shawty he'd met at the club the night of the set-up on Trigga, and ask her to come over. Kenyon had told him that Luxe was skilled as fuck with the head-game and his snitchin' ass damn sure wasn't lying.

Lloyd had been blowing up Mase's phone ever since he walked out of his condo days ago crying like a bitch because he couldn't get no weed, and Mase had yet to answer. Lloyd wasn't positive what was wrong with his dumb ass but he was sure that whatever it was wasn't something that benefitted him. So he found himself in a spot that he'd never been in before…a state of unrest.

His nerves were bad as hell because Mase was gone so he had no way of getting at Queen and no idea if she thought he was dead or not and would stop hunting him. On top of that, Kenyon was nowhere to be found but he knew the nigga was alive when he saw AK's black ass face on the late night news during a report stating a man had been found shot to death in his vehicle in Norcross. There was no report on whether a woman and her child had been found dead in the same neighborhood, so Lloyd wasn't even sure what had happened with Dior.

For the first time in his life, he wasn't sure of shit. He couldn't even confirm that Trigga was dead because of Mase's stupid ass.

That nigga gots to be the most retarded muthafucka in history, Lloyd thought to himself as Luxe slurped loudly on him. He winced a little when she gobbled his shit all the way down her throat and sucked in one of his balls. She was a pro; her ass had skills better than Superhead.

Lloyd dropped the blunt in the ashtray on the table next to him, then bit his bottom lip when Luxe started doing some shit that made him go insane every time; she would use both hands to wind his shit up like a clock while flicking her tongue back and forth across the head. The vision of her doing that, paired with the sight of her fat ass tooted in the air was just what he needed. His right leg started twitching as the biggest nut of his life started to cum upon him. Luxe opened her eyes and focused right in his as she sucked then smirked; that was enough to send him over the edge. He shot every bit of cum he could right down her throat. She covered his large mushroom head with her plump, pink lips and didn't stop sucking until she had swallowed him all up.

"GOTDAMN, you know how to do that shit!" Lloyd exclaimed when she sat up.

She licked her lips and smiled at him then rotated so she could get off the bed to grab him a warm towel. Reaching out, he smacked her on her ass and watched it jiggle as she walked away. He didn't know why, maybe it was her sex game, but a nigga felt like he was falling in love.

"Bitch, you been wit' a nigga since I met you that night?" Lloyd asked her with raised brows. He saw something pass across her eyes and he could tell she was getting ready to tell a lie.

"No, papi, I ain't fucked no nigga since I met you," she said in her high-pitch, sexy voice.

"You a fuckin' lie!" Lloyd yelled out. He reached out to grab his blunt, but Luxe must have thought he was going for a gun because she stopped and suddenly started screaming.

"NO! I PROMISE, LLOYD! I AIN'T BEEN WIT' NO NIGGA! PLEASE, DON'T SHOOT ME!"

Lloyd stopped and turned back to her with a confused look on his face. "I ain't gone shoot yo' ass for lying! You a hoe and fuckin' is what hoes do!"

Luxe calmed down instantly and bent down to pick up the rag that she'd dropped during her panic attack.

"I wasn't lyin'. I ain't fucked wit' no nigga since I met you. I was fuckin' wit' a bitch but that's it."

"Oh?" Lloyd asked with one brow raised.

Now she definitely had him feeling like he was falling in love. He placed the blunt to his lips and pulled hard, while his eyes ran down her sexy body as she wiped his dick clean. She was a little money hungry but, other than that, she gave him no problems, had fantastic head game, good pussy, *and* she was cool with eating coochie from time-to-time. She was wifey material in his eyes and he needed a replacement for Dior.

"Yeah, I was fuckin' wit' dat bitch, Tish, from the club for a little bit. She live wit' that bitch that was staring at you when I gave you my number at the club that night."

Luxe rolled her eyes as she thought back to how Keisha had been shooting her stank ass looks the night she had met Lloyd. She didn't have any issues with Keisha before that moment and had actually helped her get dressed for work that night, so it pissed her off that she was acting like a hater. Some girls danced they whole life and never were able to score a baller like Lloyd.

She felt Keisha should have been happy for her instead of acting like a bitch. But when Keisha ended up going home with the fine ass nigga that Luxe had been trying to pull, Luxe got even more heated, which was why she made sure to let herself be seen looking like a Playboy model when she was at Tish's spot and heard

Keisha's voice. She wanted to make sure that Keisha knew she couldn't measure up to shit that Luxe had going on. Luxe was the baddest bitch around and she wanted Keisha to know.

"Wait…you mean Keisha?" Lloyd said suddenly, sitting straight up in the bed. He dropped the blunt and it landed on his chest. The flame burned him and he snatched it up and began patting at his chest. When the feeling subsided, he looked back to Luxe and waited for her to answer.

"No speaky English, bitch?!" Lloyd waved in Luxe's face and she glared at him.

"What you askin' me about the next bitch for?" Luxe pouted. She sat back in the bed and crossed her arms in front of her chest. Lloyd raised his hand like he was about to smack the shit out of her and she jumped right out of her feelings and started talking.

"YES! She lives with Tish!" Luxe yelled. She backed away from him and almost fell straight off the bed in the process.

An evil grin crossed Lloyd's face as he jumped from foot to foot and threw up gang signs with his fingers, doing the EPG dance that he did when he was celebrating with his niggas. Luxe's eyes focused on Lloyd's dick as it flopped around in the air while he did his dance. Then he ran over to her, grabbed her by the sides of her face and pulled her into a passionate kiss. Afterwards, he placed his half-smoked blunt in her hand as if it were a prize. Luxe frowned at the blunt and then scrunched up her face at Lloyd.

"The hell you so damn happy for?"

"You don't even need to know. Just give me the address to where that bitch live and I'mma bring you back mo' muthafuckin' money than you ever seen in yo' fuckin' life!" Lloyd ran over to where his jeans were and started pulling them on.

"What about Tish?" Luxe asked him quietly with worry in her voice.

She felt guilty for what she was doing and hadn't called her since she started back messing with Lloyd. Part of her wanted to hear Tish's voice but she really didn't know how to tell her that she didn't have enough money to fuck with her and leave rich niggas alone. It was like the song…when a rich nigga want you, and yo' nigga can't do nothin' for ya'…bitches weren't loyal. Luxe wasn't loyal to shit she couldn't spend and that's just how it was.

"Lloyd, are you gonna hurt Tish?"

"Yeah! I'mma fuck a 'bish' up!" Lloyd exclaimed throwing his shirt over his head. He started doing his dance again all the way over to where his Giuseppe sneakers where.

"No, I said 'Tish', the girl I was fuckin' with. You gone hurt her?" Luxe shook her head but part of her wanted to laugh. She'd never seen Lloyd so excited since she had met him.

"Hell naw, as long as she stay out my fuckin' way."

"Okay," Luxe replied.

She brought the blunt to her lips and inhaled. Lloyd walked over and handed her his iPhone for her to enter the address in his GPS. She did it without another thought. He turned on his heels and bolted out of the room. There was a lot of shit going wrong in his life at the moment, but if he could fuck Keisha up for all the shit she'd done and maybe get his dope and money back, it would set things off in the right direction.

"Ay, don't forget the money!" Luxe called out to him.

He didn't answer her. Money was one thing she didn't have to worry about. As long as she kept riding with him like she had been the past couple days, she would be set for life. Dior was gone and he needed a new ride or die.

TWENTY-NINE

Mase wallowed into his roach-infested motel room and did a free-fall onto the bumpy mattress that smelled of old, bottled-up farts. If ever a nigga was in his feelings, it was Mase. He was now positively sure that he'd made the worst mistake of his life. Trigga, the only person in his life who had bothered to take care of him, was gone and now he had no one.

"My nigga only been dead for a few days!" Mase sobbed into his pillow. "What the fuck I'mma do for the rest of my life?!"

In Mase's current state of distress, it was as if he had forgotten that *he* was the one responsible for Trigga's death. He was so torn up by the mistake that he'd made that he couldn't bear to focus on the fact that he'd done something so incredibly stupid that was now affecting his entire life. He couldn't work with Lloyd any longer because the whole plan to kill his brother to begin with was tearing him apart. There was no way he could follow through.

On top of that, Queen wouldn't even answer his calls anymore and he didn't know why but he knew it wasn't good. So he chucked his brand new burner phone in the garbage outside of a restaurant downtown the first chance he got in case she was able to trace it. Then he used his last few bucks to check in to this raggedy motel in the middle of Decatur. He couldn't even afford a bus-ride home. He was at his lowest of lows.

In frustration, he reached out and banged the nightstand next to him and accidently cut on the television. Drake's voice came through the television speaker, he was singing about 'running with his woes' and the noise blared in his ears, making Mase sob even harder. The only 'woe' he'd ever had was Trigga…his brother had been his only friend and now he was gone.

Mase grabbed a pillow and covered his head with it in order to block out some of the sound but it did nothing to help him. So he reached out blindly for the remote and his hand fell upon the handle of his gun. When his finger grazed the cold metal, his cries stopped and he went completely still. An idea occurred to him in that instant and as he thought about it, it was as if everything around him went silent except for a ringing sound that echoed through his ears.

His life as he knew it was over. He had no money, no job, no skill, and no one in his corner. He was nothing without his brother. He couldn't even flag down bitches anymore. Mase had never been anything nice to look at but the money he made was enough to attract the hoes. Plus, when bitches couldn't get at Trigga, they would go to him, the next runner-up. As much as he hated that shit, he had to admit that he got a lot of pussy simply because chicks didn't like to be turned down. Trigga rejecting them always worked in his favor.

"Man, forgive me, Trigga! Forgive me, my nigga. I ain't kno'!" Mase spurted out what he'd decided would be his last words.

There was nothing more that could be done for him, so the only resolution that he could see was to put himself out of his memory and end his own life.

Sitting up on the bed, Mase wrapped his hand around the handle of the gun and lifted it in the air. The chrome glistened in the dim lighting and he squinted as he stared at it. Balancing the weight of the gun in his hand, he began to lose courage and started to think twice about his decision. Maybe he was thinking irrationally. Then his stomach growled and churned hard in his stomach, reminding him that he hadn't eaten a single thing since the day before. He thought back to days before when he saw a restaurant worker for Pappadeaux throwing out food in their large garbage dump.

Maybe I can get me some shrimps or some shit outta there, Mase thought for a brief moment.

As soon as the thought crossed his mind, his bottom lip began to tremble and fresh tears came to his eyes when he thought about how far he'd fallen.

There was no going back.

In agony, Mase banged the gun again and again on the small nightstand next to his bed, until small pieces of wood began to chip away and shoot through the air. He knew what he had to do.

With renewed courage for what was necessary, Mase raised the gun and poked the barrel inside of his mouth. He closed his eyes, commanded his breathing to slow down and made himself relax. In his mind he imagined that he would go into the afterlife, meet up with his mother who would actually love him as much as she did her other son. He imagined that she would cry at his feet and beg for him to forgive her for her wrongs. Then after he did, she would grab him and give him a hug…a real hug like she actually loved him the way he'd always wanted her to.

The room went eerily silent, even the noise outside in the hall melted away. Mase took it as a sign that he was doing the right thing. He placed his finger on the trigger and with his eyes closed tightly and his mind clear and accepting of what he knew he had to do, he squeezed.

Click!

Click! Click! Click!

Mase began to get frustrated and squeezed a few more times.

Click! Click! Clickety-click!

"Aww, HELL naw!" Mase yelled out as he pulled the gun from his mouth. He opened the chamber and checked. There were bullets inside but the gun was jammed. He must have jammed it when he was banging it on the nightstand earlier. Just his luck! He couldn't even end his life so that he could escape the hell he'd created for himself. If there was a God, it was obvious that He hated niggas.

"SHIT!" he shouted and tossed the gun to the side. It landed on the remote, making the television come on and then fell loudly to the side.

Mase groaned at the blaring noise coming from the television speakers and reached out for the remote to turn it off again, but stopped suddenly when he saw what was on the screen. The late night news was on. The news anchor was speaking about a story and next to her head was a picture of his brother, Trigga, with a headline on the photo that read "WANTED!"

"What?!" Mase shouted as he focused in on the story.

"Police are searching for this man, Maurice Bivens AKA Trigga. Bivens was arrested last Friday afternoon in connection with a double homicide that took place in his penthouse hotel room at The W in Buckhead. Bivens made bond the next day but police are looking for him in connection to another murder. Kenyon St. Michaels was found shot to death in his Buckhead condo only two days after Bivens was released from jail on bond. Police have reason to think that he may have been involved. Bivens may also have with him a small child, one-month-old Karisma Mitchell, who was not found at the scene. If you have any information on the whereabouts of Maurice Bivens or Karisma Evans, please call 1-800..."

"WHAT DA FUCK?!" Mase shouted to the top of his lungs. An angry patron of the motel, who was in the room to his right, beat on the wall to signal him to be quiet.

"Ain't nobody say shit when y'all was in there fuckin'!" Mase yelled through the wall.

There was no response. When Mase turned back to the news story, the reporter had moved on to another story about how the Lakers were recruiting some four-year-old kid named Al, a

LEO SULLIVAN & PORSCHA STERLING

basketball protégé and child genius, to play on their team when he was old enough to join the league. His mama was jumping up and down on the screen as the Laker's coach told her the news, then she scooped the little, brown-skinned boy up in her arms, planted a kiss on his forehead and hugged him tightly.

Mase watched with envious eyes and was so lost in the story that for a minute he forgot what he'd just learned. It wasn't until the four-year-old kid sunk a basket from nearly half-court that Mase remembered and jumped clear out of the bed.

"Trigga is alive..." he said slowly.

Tossing the remote onto the floor, he spun around, grabbed his empty wallet, a pack of gum to heal his grumbling stomach and picked up his faulty weapon. After securing each object into its correct location, he bolted out of the room at top speed. He didn't know exactly what it was that he was gonna do or how he had to do it, but he needed to get to Trigga and get his shit back in order with his brother. He knew now more than ever that he needed him.

He only hoped that Trigga wouldn't find out how he'd betrayed him.

THIRTY

Keisha's eyes opened suddenly when she heard what sounded like a loud bump followed by someone yelling out 'FUCK!' in the front room. After waiting for a few minutes, she decided that maybe she'd been dreaming and imagined what she thought she had heard. Tish was lying next to her, curled up in a half ball and sleeping peacefully like she didn't have a care in the world. Keisha tried to lie back down on the bed slowly so she wouldn't disturb her sleep. She knew that Tish needed it. Sleep was the best way to get over a broken-heart…unless you were like Keisha and thought about the one who had broken it in your dreams.

Closing her eyes again, Keisha tried to will herself to go back to sleep but she couldn't. The taste of alcohol still lingered on her tongue and it made her mouth feel dry like wallpaper. The sensation made her feel as if she was dehydrated and needed the biggest glass of ice-cold water she could find. Rising up slowly, she straddled Tish and then dropped her foot on the floor as she rose out of the bed. Half-way out the bed, she nearly collapsed right on top of Tish and popped her right in the face, but she just kept right on snoring. The liquor had her out like a light.

When she opened her door, she noticed that it was completely dark in the other part of the house. It was odd because her and Tish always made an effort to keep the light over the stove on so that it wasn't pitch-black in the house. Since they'd both been drinking the night before, Keisha figured that they'd probably just forgotten to turn it on.

It wasn't until Keisha started walking down the hall that she felt a chill go down her spine and her hairs raise up on her arm. It was a signal that something was wrong and she felt her heart start to beat like a drum in her chest.

But it was too late.

"Oh, you fuckin' bitches now, huh?" Lloyd's deep, icy voice cut through the silence stopping Keisha dead in her tracks.

She opened her mouth to scream but then she felt him press something hard against her back. Keisha knew what it was instantly, and her scream was reduced to a whimper as tears started to fall down her cheeks. Her worst fears were being realized. Lloyd was here and he was going to kill her.

"Where the fuck my money and shit, Keesh?" Lloyd asked, jugging the gun into her spine.

"I don't have it!" she said softly. Her head was swirling from the liquor and she felt herself wavering from side-to-side as if she wasn't standing still.

"The fuck you mean 'you don't have it'?! Did you use up all my shit?" Lloyd asked her. He grabbed her neck and squeezed tight, making her yelp.

"Answer my fuckin' question! Did you use up my shit?!"

Unable to do anything but cry silently as Lloyd stabbed her in the back with his gun and held so tightly on her neck that she could hardly breathe, Keisha nodded her head sadly. The money was gone and the dope was, too. She hadn't used it but she couldn't tell him Trigga had it. If her life had to be taken, she wanted it to be hers and hers alone. She didn't need Trigga or Tish to be involved if she could help it.

"You one dumb ass fuckin' bitch," Lloyd snarled through his teeth. "But that's okay because I'mma make you pay for that shit!"

Lifting the butt of the gun high in the air while still keeping his grip tight on Keisha's neck, he brought the gun down at top force and cracked it over the top of her head. Keisha was out immediately and went limp in his hand, making him tighten his grip on her throat. He heard a sound behind him and he released his grip on her, allowing her body to tumble to the floor. Swooping around with his gun out-stretched, he fired out a shot when he saw movement behind him.

"Keish-uhhhhh, you makin' so much damn noise. I can't sl—"

Pow!

The bullet ripped out the barrel of the gun and straight through Tish's chest. Heaving loudly with her eyes open wide as humanly possible, she placed a hand to her chest and stared at Lloyd with sheer terror etched throughout her eyes.

"Shit!" Lloyd muttered. He hadn't wanted to kill her. He made a promise to Luxe and he'd meant to keep it. He didn't want to start of his newfound relationship having to bitch-slap her ass for whining and complaining about how he'd murdered her former lover.

It's a shame, too, he thought as he lifted Keisha's limp body onto his shoulder and took a final glance back at Tish who was slumped over with her eyes closed and blood spilling out from her shoulder.

She would have been the perfect third for our threesome.

Making sure to leave the door wide open, as was the norm when an EPG ran up in a house and handled business, Lloyd walked out of Keisha's apartment, balancing her with ease. It was like toting dead weight but Keisha wasn't all that heavy to begin with. Walking out the apartment, he pressed the button to open the trunk of his brand new whip and chucked her in like she was a sack of garbage. The big body, black and blue BMW with chrome wheels was the car he'd purchased for when he needed to be low-key. But, in true Lloyd-style, he still had to make sure it was iced out.

Smiling to himself, Lloyd sat down in the driver's seat, started the car and drove off. When he got onto the main road, he turned his rap music up as loud as he could and bobbed his head happily to the music.

He didn't know how long Keisha would be out. And if she woke up before he grabbed Luxe and road out to his ranch house in Fairburn, he didn't want to hear her kicking and screaming.

THIRTY-ONE

Trigga looked down at the address he had in his hand. It was the address that he'd gotten from Cash at the club where Keisha had worked. It wasn't hard at all to get Cash to give him the number because, true to his name, Cash was all about that green and nothing else. Just like the hoes in his establishment, he could be bought for the right price.

Trigga went to the club to ask Cash if he'd seen or heard of his old friend, Lloyd, who he allowed to run drug deals through his club as long as he paid him. As Trigga expected, the first thing out of Cash's mouth was that he 'ain't see shit and ain't know shit'. Then Cash stood up to promptly walk him to the door but Trigga wasn't going to take no for an answer. After dropping three stacks on Cash's desk, his greedy face lit up and his tongue started wagging.

In a matter of seconds, he informed Trigga that Lloyd had been there the day before to pick up Luxe from work. After ranting on and on about how he was mad as hell that he would lose another good worker to Lloyd being Captain Save-A-Hoe, he handed over Luxe's address and stuffed the money in his desk drawer to signal to

Trigga that if he wanted any more information, it would cost him more.

Cash's face fell when Trigga turned sharply and walked right out of the door. Luxe's address was all he needed. He could start with her. When dealing with niggas who put pussy before business, you could bet that following the pussy would lead you right to them. It never failed.

Thinking about how women made men fall off their shit, automatically drew images of Keisha in Trigga's mind as he opened his door and sat down on his new white leather seats. He swapped his Porsche rental for a cocaine-white Audi R8 because every time he got in the Porsche, he couldn't help thinking about Keisha being in the seat next to him.

Trigga started the car, whipped it out of the parking lot and hopped on I-285 and followed his GPS to where Luxe lived. To his surprise, he quickly noticed that Luxe lived close to Keisha and he felt a tugging on his heart, while he drove the familiar route that he'd traveled down so many times on his way to her spot.

Should I... he thought to himself.

Then he shook his head 'no'. He couldn't entertain the idea that came to his mind. He had to stay focused. Frowning slightly, he narrowed his eyes and concentrated on the road as much as he could through the dark, winding roads. Although he tried to clear his mind so that he could stay focused on his business and make sure that he wouldn't fuck up what he was being paid to do, Keisha kept floating through his mind.

Against his better judgment, he let his mind wander to the last thing he'd heard her say the other day.

YOUR ASS IS RUDE!

Before he knew it, Trigga was chuckling to himself as he thought about how both of them had acted like children throwing temper tantrums. Never in his life had a woman made him as furious as she did. Never had a woman made him as happy.

Stopping at a red light, Trigga picked up his phone and looked at the text she sent him. All it said was 'likewise' but he knew Keisha enough to know that she probably wanted to tell him that she loved him, but her stubborn ass couldn't force herself to feel like she was giving in. That was something that he loved and hated about her. She was stubborn to a fault. So was he, but he was willing to go against what was natural to him for the woman he loved.

Trigga sighed and dropped the phone on the seat beside him then focused on the road. Once again his mind was clear and he was focused. He willed himself to push Keisha away at least until after he did what he had to do.

The light changed to allow the traffic perpendicular to him to turn or drive straight ahead. Trigga grunted impatiently. As late as it was, nobody should have been on the damn road. Then he saw a car that caught his attention. It was a blue and black BMW. But what made him really focus on it was the fact that the music was loud as hell. So loud that it made Trigga's chest thump as it rode by. The tints were so dark that Trigga couldn't see who was inside but something about the car was nagging at his mind.

Then suddenly he remembered what it was.

"He came round here the otha night, picked her up in some blue BWM with sparkly wheels. Not his normal flashy shit. I guess times must be hard since he got outta jail and his cousin turned rat. Maybe dat mean he won't be takin' Luxe from me after all. That bitch as greedy as they come…"

"Fuck!" Trigga yelled out.

The car had turned right off the street that Keisha lived on. Trigga's heart jumped in his chest. He'd never forgive himself if something happened to her because he wasn't there to protect her.

Without waiting for the light to change, Trigga jerked his steering wheel to the right and mashed his gas pedal. Within seconds, he was in front of Keisha's apartment. He jumped out of the car without turning it off and ran right into the house. The door was wide open and he knew from his research on Lloyd and his crew that it was what they did when they invaded a home and killed the occupants.

When he ran into the apartment with his gun drawn, the first thing he saw was blood on the wall in the hall and it was almost like his own blood froze in his veins. Then he looked down and saw a crumpled up body on the floor.

Please, God, don't let it be…

Trigga turned on the lights and let out a sharp breath when he saw the person on floor, slumped over in a way that almost seemed impossible for a person with a spine, was Tish. He made a mental note to check on her but first, he had to see about Keisha. He searched the rest of the small apartment but she was nowhere to be found. With his hands clenched to his side in grief and anxiety, he went back to Tish's body and knelt down beside her.

Tish's eyes were closed but he could tell that she was breathing faintly. She was still alive.

"Tish!" Trigga called out desperately.

He shook her slightly and felt bad for doing so. She had an injury that nearly looked fatal and he could have been doing more damage. But in his selfish state of mind, he had to try to get any information he could on Keisha. Tish's eyes fluttered when he shook her once more and she moved her mouth as if she were about to say something.

"Tish! Where is Keisha?" he asked. Trigga bit his lip as he waited for her to speak. "Is she in here?"

"No…" Tish whispered through her lips which were now a slight cool shade of blue. "Lloyd…"

Trigga released Tish from his grasp, stood up and put both hands to his temples and squeezed his eyes shut in agony when he was able to comprehend what she had whispered.

Lloyd….

Keisha was with Lloyd. She was in the car that had passed right in front of him only minutes ago. If he'd stayed focused on his mission and followed her, he would have killed Lloyd and found her.

Turning around, Trigga ran out of the house and jumped back in the car. He dialed 9-1-1, rattled off an address and threw his burner phone out the window. Hopefully someone could get to Tish in time because he had to go back in the direction that Lloyd had gone and pray that it led him to the address that Cash gave him.

He needed to find Keisha.

Trigga turned out on the main street and mashed the gas, his eyes were searching furtively for Lloyd's blue and black BMW and his ears were trained on even the smallest amount of sound that could point to where the car's location. He sped straight through all lights without caring if they were red or not. There wasn't much traffic on the road and he didn't care if there was. The woman he loved was taken and he had no idea whether she was dead or alive.

***

Detective Burns shoved the tail-end of a hotdog into his mouth and chomped angrily. This was the second one he'd eaten in less than ten minutes and he still wasn't satisfied. He was an emotional eater so when he felt frustrated on the job, he ate. It was the reason for the bulging belly he had. He'd caught his wife staring at it with disgust on more than one occasion, and it only made him eat more. It was a vicious cycle.

After the gun from Lloyd's case had mysteriously disappeared and Lloyd was let out of jail because of the illegal wire-tap, he'd been placed back on late night patrol duty. Everything Burns dreamed about at night was being pulled from his grasp and there was nothing he could do about it. No one even cared.

"I'm calling it a night," Burns said on the radio and turned on the beat up car that he'd received along with his demotion.

God, I hate my life, he thought.

"10-4, Captain. Have a good night!" Cindy said cheerfully on the other end.

Burns grunted with a deep frown on his face. He knew that she was only being nice by calling him 'captain' but for some reason he took it as a slight against him. His demotion put him even farther from his dream of rising to the top than he'd ever been. His reputation was ruined.

Just as Burns was about to make a U-turn and make the long trek home to lie in the bed with a wife who no longer desired him, he looked up in time to see an all-white sports car zoom pass him at top speed.

"What the—" Burns started.

In an instant, he pushed the button to turn on his siren and flashing lights then pulled out at high speed, right behind the vehicle. He picked up his walkie-talkie and rattled off his location and current activity to Cindy, the police dispatcher, who replied back in her normal cheerful state that she'd received the information.

"Cindy…I'm gonna need back up. You have my location?"

When Burns fell in line behind the vehicle, he noted the driver seemed to increase in speed instead of slow down. Burns grabbed hard to the steering wheel and narrowed his eyes on the target. He felt the jitters of sheer excitement in his chest; this was the most action he'd seen in a few days. The highlight of his week had been when West allowed him to tag along to arrest Maurice Bivens, who was a former suspect in a case they'd worked together a few months back. But, like that case, it seemed the case that they'd thought would really nail his ass was going to be thrown out, too.

The gun they confiscated from Maurice was clean as a shiny new whistle. And ballistics showed that it wasn't the gun which had killed the homeless couple in his room. Coupled with that, their only eye witness, the hotel's security guard, was fully convinced that Maurice was not the man he'd seen the night before in the room. When the guard supplied them with one additional detail, they discovered that their case was shot just like the ass of the man who had actually murdered the couple in the room. Maurice AKA 'Trigga' was not their man.

A few days later, Burns was told that there was now an alert issued to find Maurice for yet another murder, this time one that connected directly with the case he and West had worked months ago. But Maurice had already been released to the public on bail and there was most likely no way they would find him again. He was a smart man and Burns assumed that as soon as he knew the police were looking for him, he'd probably skipped town and become a problem in someone else's jurisdiction. Yet another opportunity escaped him.

The vehicle ahead of Burns bent corners and switched back and forth through the minimal traffic on the road in an effort to lose him. Burns kept his eyes focused on the assailant and gripped his steering wheel so tight that his knuckles turned white. He shifted his eyes only slightly when he saw his back-up approaching. He heard them shooting off coordinates back to the desk over the system in his patrol car. They were working to close the target in so he would be surrounded.

After a mere three minutes of looping around and turning down roads, Burns watched with a wide grin on his face as the white Audi finally came to a stop. They'd won. The driver was surrounded and had nowhere else to go.

"This is police work at its fucking BEST!" Burns yelled out as he prepared himself to exit his vehicle with his gun drawn.

"DROP THE KEYS OUT THE WINDOW AND EXIT THE VEHICLE WITH YOUR HANDS IN THE AIR!"

The sound of his voice booming over the speakers further excited him. There was something about the power he felt that was almost like a drug. He'd waited for this moment for so long. This was the moment that he ceased from being someone's second in command and finally was able to feel like he was the one in charge.

When West was with him, he never let him take the lead. He thought back to the moment when he could have killed Lloyd Evans, a notorious drug dealer in Atlanta, but West had batted his arm away and stolen his hopes and dreams of being recognized for taking down the leader of the notorious East Point Gang. So many times West had stolen his glory from him but in this moment, it was all about him. And even if the driver of the vehicle ahead of him was only a teenager who had snuck out and taken daddy's new ride for a spin around town, this was Burns' moment to shine.

"I REPEAT, DROP YOUR KEYS OUTSIDE THE WINDOW AND EXIT THE VEHICLE WITH YOUR HANDS IN THE AIR!"

Burns clutched tightly to his weapon and watched as the occupant rolled down his window and tossed his keys outside. Then he slowly opened the door and put one leg out the door. Burns felt his heart beating in his chest as he waited, along with his fellow officers, for the target to remove himself from the vehicle. He crept slowly to the edge of the door he was positioned behind so he could get a head start and run up on the target to handcuff him before anyone else was able to get to him.

When the man stood up out of the vehicle with his hands in the air, Burns could have pissed his pants. His face dropped and his eyes opened wide as he looked into the face of a man he recognized instantly.

Oh no! Coincidences like this just don't happen!

But it had. And right in front of Burns, standing tall with his hands in the air and a scowl on his face, was Maurice "Trigga" Bivens. The man all of Atlanta was looking for in connection to a few grisly attacks and murders. Burns could barely contain himself but he did all he could to try.

Swallowing hard, he kept his face stern and tried to conceal his joy as he ran over to complete the biggest arrest of his entire career. Maurice "Trigga" Bivens was his at last. He would rot in prison for the murders that he'd committed…maybe even get the death penalty, and Burns would be awarded by a promotion and a fat raise. And this time he wouldn't be able to wiggle out of the charges because Burns had a major piece of evidence on his side.

An eyewitness.

Thanks From THE

AUTHORS!

First, I would like to thank God for, once again, allowing me to do what I have been blessed to do and that is writing and creating with my mind and capturing the vivid imagination of millions. I would also like to thank you, the readers, without you none of this could be possible. I would also like to thank my family, which are too many to name and if I forget one cousin I'll get cursed out (LOL).

Right now, some of the most important people in my life are the team of writers on my roster. I call them Family. Shout out to the entire staff and writers at Sullivan Productions LLC Films and Literary. Also, I have to give props to my executive assistant, Tamra Simmons.

I would be remiss if I didn't thank my very beautiful and talented co-writer Porscha "Trap Queen" Sterling. For me, this has been a labor of love. We had to get our hands dirty with this installment there is so much going on with all the key ingredients you want in a novel. But, as Porscha continued to remind me, this is also a passionate love story and she made sure of that, as you will see. However, I do have to admit that one day over dinner Porscha blurted out, "I'm killing his ass!" with her eyes ablaze in fury like the characters were real! Can you guess whom she killed or wants to kill? I tried my best to talk her out of it. Now, in the next final installment, she might get her way (LOL).

Thanks for the reviews, they motivate me to write. I read them all and if you tell me to hurry, I do my best. One thing is for sure, the next installment in this series will be the last and you won't have to wait long.

So until next time, peace and blessings. And don't forget to check on my new movie, Life Without Hope.

You can follow me on Facebook or Instagram.

LEO SULLIVAN

This SURE WAS a fun book to write!

Thanks goes to my four-year-old, Al – he actually had a small cameo in this novel! Did you notice it (hee hee)?!

Thanks to the readers who lit the fire under us to get this one out! I was sick when it came close to the release date for this book and I wasn't sure we'd be able to get it out until NEXT month but you guys wouldn't let that happen! But THANK YOU for that!

Thank you to my #DOPEAUTHORS who make up ROYALTY PUBLISHING HOUSE! Without you, I couldn't have written this! You guys are so supportive with each other but also supportive of me and my dreams! I love you allllll to pieces!

Thank you so much to you, Leo! You motivate me, you inspire me, you frustrate me…you do it all because I need it all. You're the bomb.com. We argued over this book so many times but it led to a great end result. And part three…whew! It's already amazing!

THE NEXT ONE IS COMING SOON! We never make you all wait too long. But in the meantime, as you wait, check out the books written by our authors. They are some of the most talented authors who have ever done it!

I hope you enjoyed this novel. Until we meet again...#StayRoyal

Porscha Sterling

CPSIA information can be obtained
at www.ICGtesting.com
Printed in the USA
LVOW04s1323180316

479771LV00022B/420/P